C000078534

LOSING MY INHIBITIONS

FINALLY FREE AND READY TO HAVE FUN

OLIVIA SPRING

HARTLEY PUBLISHING

Dedicated to my amazing readers.

CHAPTER ONE

*A*t last.

I thought it was never going to end.

He'd been pounding away for ten minutes, grunting like a pig, and I'd been listening to the radio playing in the background, trying to figure out what advert the song before last was from. Was it the one advertising car insurance or the one for those panty liners that are supposed to keep you *cotton fresh all day long*? *It'll come to me…*

We should have just called it a night when he'd first struggled to get his machinery working. Based on tonight, it seems like what I'd read about some older men finding it difficult to get it up was true.

It was only about half an hour after he'd popped a little blue pill that he'd been able to get his little soldier to stand to attention, if you catch my drift. Which, unfortunately for me, was around the same time I started to sober up and wonder what the hell I was doing.

But by then, he was really excited, and it had been so

long since my last time that I'd got myself worked up and was just as keen as him to give it a go. I mean, when I start something, I like to see it through. *Yep, I'm dedicated like that.*

I'd also read that there are lots of benefits of sleeping with an older guy. Apparently, after years of experience in the sack, they know their way around a woman's body better than a gynaecologist, so I thought I may as well give it a try. *Purely in the name of research, of course.*

But now I was really wishing I hadn't bothered. It was about as exciting as watching a hundred-metre snail race. And this guy wouldn't know his way around my anatomy if I gave him a map.

Still, at least it was over now. I was back in the saddle. First time since I'd left my ex-husband. Frankly, I hoped it got better from here. *Please tell me it does?*

I opened my eyes slowly and glanced up at his crepey skin and flaky bald head, which had tufts of grey at the side. His droopy man boobs hung above my chest, whilst the weight of his large pot belly pressed down on my stomach.

Dear God.

I must have had a lot more to drink than I'd realised.

Don't get me wrong. If I was looking for a relationship and this was a man I'd fallen madly in love with, then I wouldn't be so shallow. It was just that right now, I was looking for fun. To make up for the years I'd wasted with my ex. When I was dreaming of the day that I'd be free from Steve and with another man, this wasn't exactly what I'd had in mind.

I'd pictured a young, hot, sexy guy with abs that would

give a Calvin Klein model a run for his money, with a full head of dark hair I could run my fingers through. A stud who would have me screaming for more, rather than wondering when it would all be over.

It was Colette, my boss, slash landlady, slash house-mate, slash friend, who'd set me up with him at my divorce party earlier this evening. Now that I was officially free, Colette said some male company might be good for me, so she'd invited Donald, her loaded sixty-two-year-old boyfriend, and he'd brought his fifty-five-year-old mate Terrence along.

I knew that I was ready to get back on the horse, and it was already under control. My cousin Alex had been helping me. She'd given me a crash course in online dating two weeks ago, and I wanted to set up my profile ASAP so I could get going on the whole swiping thing, but this big work exhibition kept getting in the way. I'd been burning the midnight oil every night and often over the weekends too, trying to get everything prepared, which didn't leave me with any time for extracurricular activities. And after another long, tiring and stressful day, a hook-up was the last thing I was thinking about. But I guess the booze I'd been drinking all night had made me relax a little too much, so when Terrence had started flirting, my libido had woken up, curiosity had got the better of me, and I'd hastily thought, *Why not just get it out the way now?*

Big Mistake.

Oh well. You live and you learn. We all do things in the heat of the moment that we regret. As long as I didn't do it again, then it was fine. Which meant I better start thinking about how I was going to get this big sweaty oaf of a man off me. *Now.* I'd heard the effects of those pills can last for hours, and I definitely couldn't endure another round.

No way.

Remind me never to drink alcohol again.

CHAPTER TWO

'There you are!' said Colette as I stepped out from the loos, tossing my long red hair over my shoulders and readjusting my black leather skirt. 'I've been looking for you everywhere!'

Blimey, can't a girl leave her desk for two minutes to answer the call of nature?

'I just had to pop to the ladies',' I said, trying to hide my irritation about having to explain myself. 'Is there something you need?'

'Yes!' Colette raised her eyebrows, her forehead barely moving. She must have had another Botox session over the weekend, as there had definitely been more movement in her face on Friday. 'I'm on my way to a lunch, but I've been double-booked, so I need you to be a darling, Roxy, and take a meeting for me.'

Not again.

Seriously. Colette was always 'double-booking' herself. You'd think she didn't have a PA or access to a calendar.

'When is this meeting?' I asked, sensing that I wasn't going to like the answer.

'Now,' said Colette.

'Now, as in *right now*?'

'Yes, darling! He's in the boardroom waiting.'

She's got to be joking. I already had a load of deadlines to meet this afternoon. She couldn't honestly expect me to drop everything because she'd been disorganised? *Who am I kidding?* This was Colette, after all.

As I thought about my to-do list, my head felt like it was about to explode.

There was less than two weeks to go until the Northern Beauty Live! exhibition in Manchester, and I was tearing my hair out. Colette had given me the sole responsibility of managing and marketing our presence at the event, and that was on top of my normal day job of running the national sales force. I was resourceful and had never been one to shy away from hard work, but frankly, expecting me to do all of this was ridiculous. Anyone with half a brain could see that this was a job for a team rather than one individual, but ever since we'd booked the space two months ago, Colette had insisted that I could do it all on my own. "You'll be fine, Roxy. I know I can trust you," she'd say.

Utter bollocks, I'd muttered to myself. *It's got sod all to do with trust, Colette. I'm not bloody Wonder Woman. There's only twenty-four hours in a day and I only have one pair of hands.*

And now she wanted to land this on me too? This was beyond unreasonable. I had been hoping to leave on time today so that I could go round to Alex's and let her finish showing me how to set up my profile on a few dating apps so that I could finally start having a life outside of work and go and enjoy some male company. If I took this meeting, I'd be stuck in the office until all hours again.

'Colette, you know that normally I'd help out,' I said, trying to keep calm. 'It's just that I've still got a load of stuff to do for the show next weekend, so I really need to focus on—'

'Don't worry about that, Roxy,' she huffed. 'I'm sure you'll find a way to get it all done. Just take this meeting for me first.'

Unbelievable. I'd have liked to tell her where to stick her bloody meeting, but after everything she'd done for me, I couldn't.

'What's the name of this guy?' I said, sighing in my head. 'What company is he from, and what's the meeting about?'

'Um,' she said, fiddling with something in her fancy handbag and avoiding eye contact. 'I think he's from a new online magazine. Wants to talk about advertising and promotional opportunities or something.'

She thinks*? Can't be that important if she's not even sure.*

'What's his name?' I repeated. 'And what online magazine is it? Just so I can research it quickly on my phone before I go in.'

'Names escape me. Just go and introduce yourself. I'm sure you'll figure it out. It'll be fine. Oh, and I said you'd give him a presentation on the company. You know, our history, who we've advertised with in the past, what's worked, what hasn't, marketing objectives for the next twelve months—that kind of thing. Best to go straight to the boardroom now, Roxy. Don't want to keep him waiting.'

Classic Colette. Not only did she dump this on me last minute when she knew I had a shitload of work to do, but she'd given me zero details and expected me to give an in-depth presentation off the cuff without having any time to prepare. But what could I do? This guy was already in the meeting room, so it would be unprofessional to send him away. I didn't want it to reflect badly on the company. If I was him, I'd hate to have had a wasted journey. It wasn't his fault she had forgotten about the meeting. And ultimately, Colette was my boss, so I didn't have a choice. Even though this was going to mess things up for me, I had to go along with it.

'Okay,' I replied reluctantly.

'Wonderful! See you later,' she said, rushing towards the door.

Not so fast...

'Er, Colette,' I called out, as I sprinted to catch her up at the exit. Running in these skyscraper heel knee-high boots wasn't ideal, but I couldn't let her leave without chasing up on getting a temp first. 'Before you go, I just wondered if there was any news on getting some help? You know, like we discussed? I've got a mountain of work to do for the show, and now I've got to take this meeting and I don't—'

'Later, Roxy.' She pushed the glass door open. '*Soon.*'

That's what she always bloody says.

'It's just you promised we'd talk about it last Monday, then again when I asked on Wednesday. And you said you'd *definitely* tell me more on Friday, but now it's Monday, another week has passed and now there's only nine working days left until the show starts and—'

'I don't have time to discuss this now,' Colette huffed. 'I've got to go. I'll be back around two-thirty. Let's speak then.'

Fobbed off again.

If it was anyone else, things would be different. At the very least she'd have hired an assistant for me from the get-go. But, because of our situation, although she'd deny it, she took advantage.

Colette and I had met years ago, when she'd come to my uni to do a talk about women in business. I'd found her really inspirational, so after the event, I'd hung around to chat to her and we hit it off. We'd kept in touch, and Colette had invited me to intern at her beauty tools company, Cole Beauty Solutions, when I graduated, which was brilliant. She gave me an assistant role and I stayed there for a few months, but back then I was young and ambitious. I wanted to travel, see the world and try different things. Colette said she thought I had potential and that there would always be a job for me if I ever wanted to return. After I got back from travelling, I worked at different companies for several years, then I met Steve and got married.

I hadn't seen Colette for almost two decades until about twelve months ago, when I'd bumped into her at the supermarket and she'd insisted we have a coffee. I remember feeling embarrassed, as I knew I looked a mess. The sparkle I used to have in my brown eyes had gone, my skin was washed out and I wasn't wearing scarlet lipstick and lashings of mascara like I always do now. I'd stopped dyeing my hair, so it was a dull, lifeless, dreary dark brown shade rather than the fiery red colour I have today, and I'd put on loads of weight. Whereas Colette was looking glamorous, as she always did. Even though I worked out she must have been in her mid-late fifties, she'd barely aged. Her shoulder-length jet-black hair was still big, bouncy and blow-dried to perfection, her make-up was immaculate and she was dressed in a signature tweed skirt suit, just like I remembered.

I told her I couldn't stay long as Steve would be back soon and expect his dinner to be ready, but we ended up chatting for ages. I don't know what came over me. Maybe it was having another woman to talk to after so long, but suddenly I broke down and found myself spilling my guts. Telling her about my controlling husband and how I was desperate to leave him, but was too afraid.

Colette, who'd recently been through a messy second divorce, said she'd help me. So for the next eight weeks, we met at the same coffee shop on a Friday afternoon and planned my escape. Colette offered to lend me the money to rent a flat to move to once I left. I refused so many times because I couldn't see how I'd be able to afford to pay her back. I had nothing. But she said I could come back to work for her just like she'd promised all those years ago. Eventually, I accepted and just before my fortieth birthday, I left Steve.

It was almost three months before I was even able to think about working. I was such a mess. At first I just used to curl up on the floor. Crying. Wondering how I'd got myself into such a shitty situation. How I'd allowed him to manipulate me. I felt so weak. I couldn't see how I would ever recover. After Colette paid for me to see a therapist, I slowly grew stronger and realised I *could* take care of myself. I'd done it before Steve, and I was determined to do it again.

I started exercising and eating healthier, so soon I was looking and feeling much better. When my confidence began to grow, I worked at Colette's two days a week, then built up to three. Two months later I was full-time, earning a salary, and arranged to start paying her back in instalments.

As the six-month rental agreement she'd secured for me was about to end, Colette suggested that rather than staying on, I should come and live with her, rent-free. That way it would be easier to pay off the money I owed her and also start saving for a place of my own.

We got on well and it made financial sense, so I'd agreed. That was seven months ago and now, a little over a year after I'd left Steve, I was doing great. Colette had given me a company car, and I had just been promoted to Sales & Marketing Manager and was really enjoying my job. Well, when I wasn't being overworked.

The problem was that Colette expected a lot, and because I knew how much she'd done for me, I felt like I could never say no to anything she asked or do anything to rock the boat. Which meant I was constantly having to work late to get everything done.

But, as I kept telling Colette, I couldn't keep doing it all on my own. I needed support. And even though she'd promised to get me an assistant to help me market our products at the show more times than I could count, yet never followed through, I'd give her the benefit of the doubt. *Again*. I mean, Colette said she'd be back at 2.30, which was only two and a half hours away, and I'd waited this long, so surely holding on for another few hours shouldn't make that much difference?

Yes. I'd trust her this time. Hopefully by 3 p.m. I'd be coming out of her office, feeling relieved to finally have an extra pair of hands. Then I'd leave at five head to Alex's and finally set up those profiles. Alex said things could happen really quickly, so who knows? If the temp started in the next few days, maybe I'd have a hot date lined up for the weekend, which would be brilliant.

For now I just had to get this stupid meeting out the way, be patient and keep my phone line clear, ready for when Colette's PA, Raquel, called me at 2.30 p.m.

Being patient? Getting a call from Raquel at 2.30? *Likely story*. It was now 4.45 and *quelle surprise*. No news on this imaginary help from Colette. I couldn't keep going on like this. That bloody meeting had eaten up two valuable hours of my day. It wasn't right.

I'd called Raquel at 3.30 and she'd said Colette was busy and would call me back in ten minutes. I'd chased again at four. She'd said she'd email me. Yet, still nothing.

Sod this waiting around. I knew Colette didn't like us going to her office unless we had an appointment, but I'd been more than patient. Especially considering how I'd bailed her out with that meeting.

I headed towards her office, expecting that Raquel would probably try and stop me, but I didn't care. I needed to get this resolved.

Result. Raquel wasn't here and Colette's door was open.

'Colette,' I said, knocking before I stepped inside.

'Roxy! Hi! How was the meeting earlier?'

'Fine. It was okay. He's going to send us a proposal next week. But that's not the reason I'm here,' I said, pulling out the pink leather chair in front of her large shiny white desk, then sitting down without waiting for an invitation to do so. 'It's about the show. The stand build is almost finished, I've ordered a mixture of our bestsellers to retail on the stand, including the facial cleansing brushes, tweezers and gel manicure kits, and the stock should arrive at our office by Friday. Maggie and Jeremy are confirmed to work on both days to take the orders, so that's all in hand, but as I've mentioned, I've still got a load of stuff to do, like checking over the brochure proofs before they get printed, managing the social media and a *mountain* of other things. I just don't see how I can get it all done in time by myself.' I winced.

'Don't worry,' Colette said in her calming voice. 'It will all work out in the end. I have faith in you,' she said.

'That's the thing, though, Colette. It won't be fine. Not unless I get some help. I know you have confidence in me and I'm grateful for that, but I'm telling you, this is all going to go tits up…' I paused, reminding myself that despite our relationship, I needed to be professional and not let the words in my head come out of my mouth without toning them down first. 'Sorry. Let me rephrase: I'm very concerned that things will go *badly wrong* with this show if I don't get some support. *Right now*. There's just too much to do. You mentioned last Wednesday that you had something in mind that would help and would tell me more about it last Friday?'

'Yes!' She beamed. 'I do indeed! *Awww.* Won't you

just look at him!' She turned one of the many silver picture frames cluttering up her desk around to face me. 'Isn't he just adorable?'

Oh, here she goes again, harping on about her bloody son. Honestly! You'd think he was the baby Jesus the way she goes on about him. As I stared at the photo with his buck teeth, train track braces, teenage spots, glasses, greasy hair and horrendous clothes, it took every ounce of willpower for me to resist the temptation to say, 'No, not really,' but thankfully my normally absent filter prevented those words falling out of my mouth just in time.

I know people think their kids are the most perfect things that graced the earth, and even though I don't have or want any children myself, I get it. I really do. Colette had carried him for nine months. Nurtured him. It was natural for her to think he was amazing. But at the same time, let's get real. In no universe would her son be considered cute. And I'm not being mean. A lot of teenagers look gawky at that age. Myself included. *Christ.* I remember some really shocking photos of me from my school days, which were probably much worse than his.

Aaargh! If only I could just say what was in my head, things would be so much easier. Instead, I was sitting here wracking my brain for something polite to say— which was for the best, as I didn't want to upset Colette. But it was just that after years of having to hold my tongue, now that I was finally free to speak my mind, having to be careful with my words and not say what I felt was *not* coming easily.

'Well, he's, erm…he's…he's certainly your son!' I said, straining a smile. *This is* so *awkward. How the hell did we even get on to speaking about him anyway? Hello.*

Priorities? 'Erm, Colette, you were talking about getting some support, to help me for the show?'

'Yes! Yes, I was! And here it is!' She grinned.

What's she on about? Clearly Colette's lost the plot.

'Sorry, Colette. I don't follow?'

'Finn!' She grinned again. 'My baby! My baby boy is finally coming over to see me! And to help *you*!'

'What?' I frowned.

'Just what I said! Finn will be here in the office from tomorrow to help you prepare for the show. He's got lots and lots of experience. Used to help me out here in the school holidays. He'll be amazing, I just know it! Isn't it *wonderful*?'

Oh dear God.

As she clapped her hands like an overexcited seal, my stomach sank. *That's* the support I'd be getting? From her *son*?

Jesus fucking Christ!

Her idea of 'support' was bringing in some entitled brat? *Lots of experience my arse. There go her rose-tinted glasses again.* Probably never worked a day in his life. Helping out in the holidays hardly made him a marketing genius. He'd definitely be a spoilt, stuck up wanker. I just knew it. Even though I remembered her saying he had gone to live in America with his dad a few years ago, you could tell she still thought the sun shined out of his back-side. Not only was her desk covered with his baby and school photos, but the walls in the hallway in her house were like a Finn museum and there was a shrine of his pics in the living room too. Creepy if you asked me.

This wasn't going to be helpful or supportive. It was going to be a *disaster*. I was already short of time and now

I was going to have to spend it hand-holding and showing him how to use a photocopier, as he'd probably never seen one in his life, wiping his snotty nose and explaining things over and over again. I just didn't have the patience. I'd probably end up screaming and calling him a useless dickhead in front of the whole office. I knew I would. And then I'd get the sack for daring to raise my voice at her golden child. This was going to be a shitstorm of epic proportions. I could just see it.

'Erm, Colette…' I said, digging deep for some diplomacy, 'that's a really sweet idea. It's just that I need someone that can hit the ground running—*sprinting*, in fact—and so I just don't know if, erm, if your son will, erm…will…' *Bloody hell*. I was useless at this subtlety stuff. 'What about that intern we had here when I started? Kimberley? It's been a few weeks since I last contacted her to check her availability, so I could try calling her again. She might be free now. She was really good.'

'I won't hear of it!' Colette folded her arms. 'It's all settled. Finn's been staying with my sister in Paris for the last few days and his ticket to London is all booked, ready for him to arrive here in the office from 9 a.m. sharp tomorrow to help you. He's *very* excited, and I know you'll take him under your wing and show him the ropes, won't you, Roxy? I trust you. It will all be fine. I cannot *wait* to see my little baby! It's been *so* long!' She picked up the frame, clutching it tightly to her chest. Any minute now she'd probably start showering the photo with kisses and trying to pinch his cheeks like he was really here.

'Anyway!' She jumped up from her chair and grabbed her black handbag from the table. 'Must dash. I have a meeting with a supplier in town and then I'm out for dinner with Donald, so I won't be home until late. Actually, could you be a darling and pick up some organic smoked salmon and a packet of gluten-free bagels from the supermarket on your way home? Just in case Donald stays over for breakfast? Wonderful! Oh, and be sure to have everything set up on the spare desk for Finn to start tomorrow, won't you? See you later, darling.'

And with that she was gone.

That meant, as well as babysitting the spoilt brat, now I had to set up his desk for him too? As if I didn't already have enough to do.

So much for leaving on time, lining up a date for the weekend and having some fun.

Just when I'd thought my day couldn't get any worse, it had.

CHAPTER THREE

'I'm offended!' said Alex, taking a gulp of her rosé.

Even though I still had a shed load of work to do after setting up Finn's desk, by 7 p.m. I was so pissed off I'd decided to pack up, leave the office and drive to South London to Alex's flat. As it took so long to get here and back from where I was in North London, and I still needed to go to the supermarket to pick up Colette and Donald's breakfast for tomorrow, we wouldn't have enough time to set up my dating profiles, which was annoying. But I thought it was worth the journey, because at least I could sit with her for an hour and let off some steam.

'Offended?' I frowned. 'Why?'

'That I didn't get an invite to your divorce party!'

'Oh *please*! You should be thanking me. It was about as exciting as a wake! Colette just ordered in some Chinese and we had a couple of bottles of bubbly. Actually, that's probably what I drank by myself to numb the boredom of having to talk to Donald's friend, who she set me up with.'

'Ooh, *exciting*! Alex gushed, twirling her long choco-late-brown hair around her fingers. *Looks like she'd just had her extensions reapplied.* She must have got back from work late too, as she was still wearing her high-waisted grey pencil skirt and tight white top. 'A new love interest! So, do you reckon he could be a potential contender to help you get back in the saddle again?'

'Already done…' I raised my eyebrows. 'I overdid it on the Prosecco and ended up bonking him upstairs at the end of the night. It was *awful*.'

'Oh shit!' Alex covered her mouth with her hand in shock. 'Sorry to hear that, Rox.'

'Tell me about it. But *whatever*. At least I dusted off the old cobwebs. Would have preferred some fresh meat rather than a leathery slab of overcooked rump, but hey ho.'

'Rox, you are *terrible*! You can't say that! Imagine if a man said that about a woman!'

'I don't give a toss, Alex. And men *do* talk about women like that. All the time. Why are women always supposed to be so meek and prim and proper? It's just us girls talking. I wouldn't say that to his face. *Obviously*. It's just personal taste. Nothing wrong with that.'

It's true. Some women are attracted to younger guys, whereas others like someone more vintage. Take Colette, for example. She'd already asked me twice about whether I was going to see Terrence again, even though I'd told her on Saturday morning that I wasn't, and she was always harping on about the joys of dating an older man. "Don't be bothering with men in their forties," she'd say. "They're still finding their feet, working on their issues, dealing with their first ex-wives and feeding their kids.

You need a *mature* man. A man in his fifties, sixties or even seventies, who has lived and experienced life. A man that has spent decades working hard, making his mark, who is ready to enjoy the fruits of his labour and wants to share that with someone. And a man who has picked up a lot of tricks on how to please a woman along the way…" She'd grinned.

I heard what she was saying and it *did* make sense. *In theory.* But I just didn't feel like that was what *I* wanted. Even though Terrence was just one guy and I hadn't been with a younger, older or *any* other man since I'd got hitched twelve years ago, going for a sugar daddy wasn't going to float my boat. Personally, I'd prefer someone in their early to mid-thirties.

Mmm. Yes…

I closed my eyes and pictured a topless hunk in tight little boxer shorts and instantly felt my heart beating faster.

'No! I'd like a toy boy,' I said, slamming my hand on the reclaimed pine kitchen table. 'Someone a few years younger than me, that doesn't look like a bloated, wrinkly raisin with wiry grey pubes. Y'know. Someone who's fit and *oh so fuckable*…'

'Cousin: you never cease to shock me!' chuckled Alex, standing up to get a tube of Pringles out of the rustic blue kitchen cupboard, then sitting back down.

'Don't get me wrong. I appreciated the gesture. Throwing a party was kind of Colette, but if she *really* wanted to help me celebrate my divorce, I'd rather she'd hired a strippergram. Now *that* would have been worth celebrating!' I cackled.

'*Ah!* It's so nice to hear you laughing again, Rox. It's like the old you is slowly coming back! I've missed you.'

'I've missed me too,' I said, filling my mouth with a few crisps. 'It's been too long.'

'It has! On a more serious note, though,' said Alex, softening her voice, 'how are you feeling? Now that the divorce is official?'

'Relieved,' I sighed. 'Like a weight has been lifted off my shoulders. The sixth of September. I'm going to always remember the date everything was finally confirmed. Honestly, Alex, I never thought that day would come.'

'Yeah, he really tried to drag it out for as long as he could, didn't he?'

'Yep. Even now, I still can't believe that the arsehole tried contesting the grounds for divorce. What a joke! It was so obvious that his behaviour was beyond unreasonable.'

'Crazy that he tried to refuse signing the papers too.'

'I know! And when he did, he'd deliberately taken as long as he could. It was all an ego thing. He just didn't want to get the blame.'

'Dickhead,' said Alex.

'Tell me about it. And it's annoying because I probably would have been entitled to a settlement or something from him, but I didn't go down that route because I thought it would make the process faster. Especially considering there were no children involved or other financial agreements to sort out. But of course, Steve being Steve still found a way to drag his feet and make it as messy and as long as he could. At least it's over now, though. I've got peace of mind. We've cut all ties, and I never want to see or hear from him ever again. I'm finally free.'

I started thinking about those dark days with Steve.

We'd met in a pub when I was twenty-nine and in the midst of a *where is my life going?* crisis. All of my friends were getting married and starting to have kids and I'd panicked. Back then, I thought that was what I wanted too and what was expected of me. I felt like if I didn't settle down by the time I was thirty, I'd be a failure. So when Steve had asked to marry me just three months after we'd started dating, I'd said yes straight away.

In the beginning, he was charming and showered me with attention and compliments. I was chuffed when he said he loved me so much that he didn't want us to wait to tie the knot and that we should just do it at a registry office without any friends and family. He told me it would be exciting. And I believed him. *Idiot.* We got married three weeks later. Little did I know that it was one of the first signs of his mission to control me.

'I can't even begin to tell you how much of a relief it is,' I said, taking a cheeky sip of her wine. I could really have done with a drink right now, but as I had to drive home, I'd settled for a Diet Coke instead. 'I feel good. *Really great.* I've been rebuilding my life slowly this past year and I'm definitely a million times stronger than I was when I left him, but now everything's official, it just feels like I can finally start over. *Properly.* Think about getting my own place one day.'

'Yeah, can't be easy living and working with your boss 24/7,' said Alex.

'It's okay,' I replied. It wasn't so bad sharing Colette's house. Even though she constantly asked me to run errands for her and I had to follow her rules, which, whilst under-standable, was a bit like living back with my parents again, at least there was plenty of space. I had my own bedroom and bathroom, and when I got home from work, Colette was often out at dinner with suppliers or with Donald. Then at weekends, she'd either stay over at his place or fly off somewhere on his private plane. *Oh, how the other half lives.* And of course there was the big advantage of not having to pay rent.

'We get on well, most of the time, and respect each other's space, so it's fine. Now I just need to start enjoying life a bit more.'

'Cheers to that!' said Alex, clinking my glass. 'I can't wait until you finally get your own home. And as great as it is to see you building your career, I'm glad you're finally ready and open to putting yourself out there romantically again. Speaking of which, have you set up your profile on any of the dating apps I showed you?'

'No, not yet. I was hoping to get here earlier so that you could have helped me do it this evening, but all this work and preparing for the exhibition keeps getting in the way.'

'It's been nuts from our end too,' Alex huffed. 'Really glad that you're involved, though. Thanks again for booking. My Steve—*ugh*, let me rephrase as that sounds hideous, like we're an item or something. What I mean is my *boss* Steve, as opposed to your ex Steve, was really happy to have your company on board as a new client, which is no mean feat as he's never happy about anything.'

'Well, you did give us a nice, juicy discount on the stand space too, so thanks again for that. Shame the show's going to be a total shit-fest for us, though.'

'What?' Alex frowned. 'Why do you say that?'

'How long have you got…?' I groaned before filling

her in on my conversation with Colette and her ridiculous idea to bring her son in to help.

'Well, you never know. Maybe it won't be so bad. As long as he knows how to make coffee, that'll be at least one task ticked off your daily to-do list,' she laughed.

'Not funny! He probably doesn't know how to do that either. Anyway, talking about it is only going to depress me more, so let's change the subject. Why don't you tell me all about your latest dating escapades?' I said, rubbing my hands together. 'That'll *definitely* entertain me…'

I stepped out of the shower and exhaled. I'd had a lovely evening with Alex. Because my ex had cut me off from everyone, up until recently, I hadn't seen her in years. We'd always got on like a house on fire, especially in our teens, and she was the only family I'd contacted since leaving Steve.

Sounded so silly now. How could I let a man stop me, a grown woman, from doing what I wanted? Why hadn't I just told him to sod off and gone to see or talk to Alex anyway? But when you're in it, it's not that simple. He'd bought us a house in Milton Keynes and, after we got married, convinced me to give up my job at the marketing agency in London because of the two-hour commute each way. And before I knew it, Steve had somehow transformed me from a confident, outgoing career woman to an obedient housewife. I was brainwashed.

He'd gradually chipped away at me and my confidence. I'd become weak, mentally and physically. Whilst I could clearly see now that the marriage was toxic, at the time, I was just on autopilot. Doing whatever I was told. It made my blood run cold just thinking about it. Thank God I was out of that now.

Just as I started drying myself off, I heard a loud bang downstairs.

What the…?

Sounded like it came from the kitchen. Could Colette have come home whilst I was in the shower? I looked at the clock on the wall. 10.37 p.m. When she went out with Donald, she didn't normally get home before eleven. I crept across the soft cream carpet in the hallway to the spare bedroom, which overlooked the lush, perfectly land-scaped front garden and the grand light grey paved drive-way. The Audi Colette had given me as a company car was there, along with her Range Rover, but not the Mercedes she used for work. Maybe she'd had a drink and Donald had dropped her home?

No. Something didn't feel right.

I heard another crash. Like a pan dropping on the floor.

Shit. Must be an intruder.

I headed back to my bathroom, wrapped a towel around me and searched for a 'weapon'. The solid silver free-standing toilet roll holder was the biggest and heaviest thing I could find. *That'll do.*

I clutched it tightly and crept down the wide marble staircase and across the white-and-grey marble floor in the large dark hallway, stopping outside of the sliding glass double kitchen doors, then poking my head slowly around the corner.

I knew it. I knew it wasn't Colette.

I squinted as I tried to make out the figure at the back of the kitchen.

I could see someone climbing through the window. From what I could make out from his silhouette, half of his body had made it onto the black granite worktop, but he'd knocked off some of the pots resting beside the stainless-steel kitchen sink in the process and was now trying to drag the rest of himself inside.

Bastard.

Sensible Roxy knew I should call the police, but she was quickly being overruled by *irrational adrenaline junkie Roxy*. How dare this bum try and break into Colette's home? She'd worked damn hard to buy this fancy five-bedroom house and he thought he could just come in here and steal her stuff?

And anyway, even if I *did* call the police, by the time they got here, if they even bothered to turn up, he'd be long gone. Off trying to break into some other innocent person's home. What if next time it was a little old lady who couldn't defend herself and he ended up running off with her life savings? Or worse, what if he pushed her to the ground and killed her? *These people make me sick.* He was just another bully. Like Steve. Well, I wasn't having it! Someone had to stick up for hardworking, decent people and confront these thugs.

Just as he slid the rest of his body onto the worktop and jumped down onto the glossy charcoal tiled floor, I found myself flicking on the light switch and charging at him like a gladiator, swinging the toilet roll holder above my head, then whacking him on the back.

'What the hell!' he shouted, looking startled as I struck him again. 'Stop! What are you doing?' he yelped as I swung at him once more. This time he reached up, grabbed the holder before it struck his body and effortlessly took it out of my hands like I was holding on to a tiny pencil. 'Stop trying to attack me, you crazy woman! I live here!'

What?

I froze and jumped back. *He lives here? No, he bloody doesn't. I live here. With Colette.* That must be a trick these burglars used to throw you off guard when they get caught. Well, I wasn't falling for it. I should be careful, though. What if he tried to attack me? My heart was pounding so fast. I grabbed a heavy frying pan off the counter and lifted it above my head, ready to take a swing at him again.

'For God's sake! Put the frying pan down! Honestly, I just forgot my keys. That's why I climbed through the window. I mean, do I look like a burglar to you?'

I stepped back again and looked him up and down.

Well, he wasn't wearing a balaclava or gloves, so he'd have to be pretty stupid to break into a house with his face exposed and put his fingerprints everywhere. But these criminals are much bolshier these days. They know the police don't have the resources to work on burglaries, so they don't need to worry about getting caught. He was probably an opportunist who saw that the window was open and thought he'd try his luck.

I looked at him again, scrutinising him from top to bottom.

Holy shit. He's H-O-T.

Around six foot three, with short dark, slightly wavy hair, neatly trimmed beard and dark brows. Even though his deep brown eyes were currently bulging out his head from fear of me cracking it open with this pan, they still looked sparkly. And his chest. Those broad shoulders, and *good Lord*, look at those biceps. *Wow.* They were bulging out of his tight black jumper, and don't even get me started about what he looked like he was packing in the lower body area.

Sweet Jesus.

Hold on.

What the fuck was wrong with me? He was a criminal who'd just broken into Colette's home, and rather than figuring out how I was going to stop myself from getting murdered, I was busy undressing him with my eyes. *Get a grip, woman.*

But he was right. He really *didn't* look like a burglar. Not like the ones you see on TV. Surely with a face and body like that, he could earn a living from modelling, not from breaking into people's homes? I found myself lowering the frying pan as my resolve began to weaken. He was far too handsome to be a criminal…

Stop being so ridiculous. The facts were clear. He was an intruder. *Don't let him fool you.* I swung the frying pan in the air again.

'Honestly! There's been a misunderstanding!' he shouted, raising his hand to grab the pan from me.

'Misunderstanding my arse! I need you to put the toilet roll holder on the floor, then put your hands behind your back and lay down in front of me. *Do it!* Before I knock you out, you thieving bastard!' I said, swinging the pan like a tennis racket and jumping up and down like a boxer in a ring in an attempt to look threatening. *That'll get the adrenaline pumping through my body again.*

Yes. Once he was on the floor, I could grab a tea towel or something from the counter and wrap it round his hands. Probably wouldn't be long enough, but I'd work it out. Then put something round his feet too. After that I could lock the window back, run into the hallway, grab my phone from my bag and *then* I'd call the police. I'd also take a photo of his face. Gorgeous or not, if he *did* manage to escape, at least I'd have his mugshot and they could put it in the paper or on their most wanted list. They'd soon catch up with him. *Good plan.* Watching all those crime series on TV when I was trapped inside that prison of a house was finally paying off.

'On the floor. *Now!*' I said in my best scary cop voice as I jumped up and down again. '*Move!* You've messed with the wrong woman, sunshine!'

'Okay, okay,' he said, maintaining eye contact and then smiling. *What a weirdo. Probably gets a kick at doing this kind of shit.* 'I'm putting the toilet roll holder down as requested, and I'll lay down too if it makes you happy. Although, you might want to pick your towel up from the floor first...'

You have got to be joking...

Shit.

I glanced down to see the white towel in a heap. *Fuck.* I was standing there stark raving naked with everything on show. In front of the hot burglar.

Mortified.

I swiftly picked up the towel and wrapped it around me tightly. *Bollocks.*

'Not that I'm complaining, of course,' he smirked, 'as I've got to say, the view is *spectacular*. But it's just that if I'm laying on the floor in front of you and you're planning to straddle me and tie me up in some way, which of course I wouldn't object to—well, when my mum gets home, then she might get the wrong idea and it could make things a little awkward...'

His what?

His *mum*?

I heard the key go in the door and Colette's footsteps approaching.

'And looks like she's here now…' he said, folding his arms smugly.

'Baby?' she shouted, her footsteps quickening. 'Baby, is that you?' She rushed into the kitchen, barged past me and threw her arms around him. 'My darling! I wasn't expecting you until tomorrow morning! Sorry, I only just saw your text saying you'd forgotten your key.'

'Hi! No worries. Yeah, I know. I took an earlier Eurostar,' he said, resting his hand on her back and patting it gently.

'Look at you!' she gushed, planting a big kiss on his cheek. 'As handsome as ever!'

This can't be happening…please don't tell me…

'I see you've met my lovely Finn,' she beamed, stepping back to admire him, glancing at me and then throwing her arms around him again.

Finn?

This was Finn?

This was her son?

But he was a *man*. A big, strapping, hot hunk of a man.

I don't get it. The way she spoke about her 'baby boy', I thought he was still a child. A teenager. At a push, perhaps he was in college. The photos. On her desk. All around the house. They were all *baby* photos. Young *boy* photos. *Teenage* photos. Not *man* photos. He had to be—what, in his mid to late twenties? I couldn't speak.

'Yes, Mother,' he smirked as she closed her eyes and rested her face on his shoulder. 'I've already become acquainted with your houseguest. I must say, she gave me *quite* the welcome…'

Cringe…

'I'm so happy to hear that, darling. I'm glad that you're home.'

'Yes,' he continued, 'it was very unexpected as I didn't realise you still had someone living here. There were no lights on. I even tried ringing the doorbell and there was no answer. But I must say, after the warm reception I've just received, I'm very excited to be here too. I think this is going to be a very enjoyable trip.' He winked as he looked me up and down, then licked his lips. '*Very* enjoyable indeed…'

Oh God. I think I'm about to die from embarrassment.

Ground, please swallow me up.

Now.

CHAPTER FOUR

That's all I need.

I'd left the house at the crack of dawn to avoid having to sit across the kitchen table eating breakfast with Colette and Finn—her bloody *son*—but it seemed they'd decided to have an early start too, as Colette's Mercedes had just pulled into the car park. He got out and was now heading towards the office.

To say that today was going to be awkward was an understatement. How was I supposed to look him in the eye, never mind work opposite him, knowing he'd seen me naked? It wasn't that I was ashamed of my body. I'd worked damn hard for months to get myself back in shape and finally learn to love it. It was just that, now that I did, I'd like to choose how, when and *who* I showed it to.

I placed my head in my hands and winced as flash-backs of me swinging the frying pan at him came flooding back, followed by Finn smirking after he'd dropped the bombshell that my towel was on the floor. *Christ.*

'Hey, Roxy!' Finn said, striding through the office

door. I was the first one here, so the office was silent, and his deep voice echoed through the room. 'It *is* you, isn't it?' he smirked. 'Didn't recognise you with your clothes on…' He chuckled. I wanted to slap him. 'Don't worry,' he said, resting his large hand on my shoulder, 'let's forget it ever happened. If I'd known you were still living there, I would've kept ringing the bell until you answered. Would have saved me having to carry my suitcase to the garden, climb through the window, and of course I could have avoided getting whacked by you. *Ouch.*' He rubbed his back, feigning pain. 'That's some swing you've got there. Do you play tennis? *No?* Golf?' He laughed again.

Dickhead.

I stared him straight in the eyes. I didn't say a word, but with a face like thunder, my expression was saying, *Don't fuck with me, arsehole.*

I pushed my chair back and stood up in front of him. *Gosh, he's tall.* At least a foot taller than me. My head literally only reached his chest. He was wearing smart navy trousers and a white shirt which clung to his solid torso, and annoyingly, I was finding it hard to take my eyes off it.

Focus. Focus. Focus.

We'd already had an embarrassing start, and if I didn't put my foot down now, he'd think he could continue with this bantering, and I wasn't having it.

'Look, *Finn.* This might be some little holiday for you, but while you're here, sitting at that desk, you're here to work. Understand? We've got a lot to do, so cut the joking around and focus, okay? Last night was a misunderstanding, pure and simple. Yes, I thought you were a burglar, and I'm sorry I hit you, but I was trying to protect your mum's house. And, *yes*, my towel dropped on the floor. *Big deal.* I'm sure you've seen a naked woman before, so get over it.'

I wished *I* bloody could. I sounded confident, I *think*, but inside I was still mortified.

'Not a body like that, I haven't.' He smirked again. All this smirking and showing off his cute dimples was starting to annoy me. I glared at him and put my hands on my hips. 'Erm, sorry,' he said. 'Inappropriate. Got it. Absolutely. I'm here to work. Last night was a misunder-standing. I totally agree, Roxy. Won't mention it again. And don't worry, whilst I'm at work, I promise to try and be the consummate professional. Mum's filled me in on the show and how much you need my help, so whatever you want me to do to you—I mean, *for* you—I'll jump right on it.' There was that smirk again.

Aaaarrgggh. Dammit.

Colette was right. Her son *was* cute. How had the boy in that photo transformed into a god like him? *Unbeliev-able.* His skin was amazing. His eyes. His juicy lips. I still didn't understand why she only had pictures of him as a boy and not more recent ones of him as a man. Strange.

Look at his body. I really loved his sense of style too… *Gosh.* I was staring at him. *Again.* I needed to stop this. Finn was my assistant. Temporary assistant. And Colette's son. He was here to work. *Just to work.* Nothing more. And we had a lot to do. I couldn't waste time ogling him. I was a professional. Just to clarify: a professional manager. Not a professional ogler. Although if I kept on like this…

'Glad to hear you're taking this seriously,' I said, standing up straighter and regaining my composure. 'Okay, so you'll be sitting here.' I pointed to the glossy white desk opposite mine. He pulled out the pink leather chair and sat down. *Yes, pink.* Colette reckoned that they brightened up the place. Although it was a bit too Barbie for me, I suppose it was *different* to the standard black chairs that you normally find in offices. It fitted nicely with the white walls, wooden flooring and sleek modern interior. 'I've put a pad here for you and printed out some notes on what's been done so far, and I thought we could start by running through some of the key tasks we need to get signed off in the next couple of days.'

'Sure,' he said, taking his phone from his pocket and tapping away.

'Er, hello? Finn? Now's not the time to be texting your friends!' I huffed.

'No, of course not. I was just bringing up notes on my phone. I prefer to write on here rather than on a pad. It's a little, er, old school.'

Smart arse. Is he saying I'm old? I suppose I must be to him.

'*Whatever.* As long as the work gets sorted, I don't care what you use. So here's what I need you to do…'

I briefed him on the most important tasks as he stared at me. *Bloody hell, he's intense.* It was like he was looking into my soul. I felt like I was naked all over again. I looked away, reminding myself to focus and try to keep calm.

'So what other marketing have you got in place?' asked Finn.

'What do you mean?' I frowned.

'Like, to draw customers to the stand?'

'Well…I…I booked an ad in the show guide…' I stuttered.

I hadn't got anything else in place. When would I have

had the time to do that? That was why he was here. *To help me.*

'No competition or prize draw?'

That was a good idea, actually. Wish I'd thought of that. My brain had been too fried.

'Yes, please look into that too. Anyway,' I said, trying to regain control and not sound like I was incompetent, 'the brochure is top priority for today. It's ready to go. Just give Tony the printer a call and tell him we need five thousand copies. This is the name of the company, and here's his number,' I said, scribbling it down on a Post-it note.

'Thanks.'

'Any questions? Clear on what you need to do?'

'Nope. Crystal. CID.'

'CID?' I replied. *Why's he mentioning the Criminal Investigation Department?*

'Sorry, bad habit. It means *Consider It Done*.' He smiled. *God, he's got lovely teeth. Those braces really were worth it...*

For goodness' sake! So much for focusing.

'Good,' I said, bringing professional Roxy back in the building. He *seemed* to understand. Well, he made all the right noises. But time would tell. *Let's see if he actually gets the job done...*

It was now coming up to 2 p.m. Almost six hours since I'd briefed Finn, and he hadn't made a single phone call. He occasionally tapped away on his keyboard and stared at the screen a lot, but for the past hour, all I could hear was his phone pinging, and then he'd keep loudly typing out a reply. *Bet he's messaging some woman.* Actually, more like a string of women. *I wonder if he has a girlfriend or multiple fuckbuddies over here? Probably.* Anyway, it was pissing me off. I'd tried to hold back from micromanaging, but I needed to know what he'd been up to. I decided I'd go to the loo and check his screen on the way back.

Quelle surprise! What was golden boy doing? Ogling some half-naked woman's photo whilst scrolling through Facebook. *Brilliant. Just bloody brilliant.*

I slumped down at my desk. *Screw it.* I wasn't putting up with him surfing the internet and texting girls when there was work to be done.

'How's it going?' I raised my eyebrows.

'Huh? Oh, it's going great actually,' he said, eyes still fixated on the screen.

'Really? So have you called—' Just as I was about to chase him on the printers, Colette interrupted.

'Darling, get your coat. We're leaving…'

'What?' I snapped. 'But there's still so much to do, and Finn has to…'

'Sorry, Roxy, he'll work late tomorrow. I need him to come with me. *Right now.*' Finn frowned as he looked up at Colette, then picked up his coat. 'Actually, Roxy, can you be a darling and cancel my dinner with that supplier I'm supposed to be meeting tonight? If you look through my emails, their name will be there. *Somewhere.* Oh, and could you be a love and put together a little list of our top ten bestsellers in Scotland in the last six months and email it to me by 7 a.m. so I can read over it whilst I have breakfast tomorrow, ahead of my meeting? I'm sure it won't take you long. See you later, darling,' Colette said as she breezed out of the office, with Finn beside her.

Is she serious? I was already struggling to do my own work and now she'd just dumped more shit on me at the last minute. *So typical of her.* And neither of those tasks were five-minute jobs. I knew from experience that her emails were completely disorganised and Raquel wasn't in today, so it'd take me ages to go through all of them to find out who she was talking about. Why didn't she just write their details in a diary or calendar like normal people?

I'd need time to collate those sales figures too. And then there was all the work that Finn hadn't done this afternoon. *This is a joke.*

So was this how it was going to be? Him spending all morning on social media and then just swanning off with his mum in the afternoon? This was *exactly* the kind of shit that I thought would happen.

Well, I wasn't standing for it. Finn and I were going to have words when I got home.

It was Wednesday morning and I was still fuming. I hadn't finished work until ten last night. And can you believe Finn and Colette still weren't home when I got back. Whilst I was in the office working my arse off, they'd pissed off without a care in the world. Colette was probably showing him off to Donald or had taken her golden boy on a fancy shopping trip. *So selfish.*

I glanced at my phone. It was 7 a.m. If I hurried up and finished my breakfast, provided there was no traffic on the roads, I might be able to get into the office by 7.30. *God knows what time Finn will decide to make an appearance.* I'd crashed out just before midnight and there was still no sign of them. So now he was probably going to call the office and say he was too tired to start on time and then crawl into work at noon because Colette let him do whatever he wanted. *Lazy fucker.*

I took another spoonful of yogurt. Suddenly I heard the front door slam and in came Finn. He was wearing a pair of shorts and a tight vest and was dripping with sweat.

And, yes, he did look hot. In every sense of the word.

'Morning, Roxy.' He grinned. *Oh, his smile…*

What's wrong with me? I was supposed to be angry with him. *Remember?*

Don't you bloody good morning *me*, I said in my head as I tried to regain focus. 'I need to talk to you, Finn.'

'Sure,' he said, gasping for air. 'Can I at least get a glass of water first?' He strolled over to the fridge, pulled out a bottle of water and took a large gulp. '*Whoo!* Think I pushed myself too hard on my run. It's so hot in here!' How did he even have the energy to go for a run considering they'd got back so late?

He started peeling off his vest to reveal the most magnificent chest. Each and every one of his gorgeous abs looked like it had been carefully chiselled out of marble, and there was a thin trail of dark hair leading from his belly button down to the top of his shorts.

Oh. My. God.

As he tossed his head back and the drops of water slid from the bottle and caressed his chest, it was like I was watching a *Men's Health* front cover photo shoot in slo-mo. *Look at those abs.* Those muscles. *Everything…*

I will not be distracted. I will not be distracted…

After all those years of having Steve's sweaty body on top of me, I should have been turned off by the sweat sliding from his face, past his broad shoulders and running slowly down his chest. So why was I feeling like I just wanted to lick it off every inch of his body instead?

I wonder what he tastes like. I wonder what he feels like?

God, am I dribbling? Please tell me I'm not. I was mad at him for flaking on me yesterday. For swanning off early. And for not doing his job whilst he was there. I shouldn't be standing here gawping.

'So, you were saying you wanted to talk to me about something?'

'Huh?' I said coming out of my trance and pushing the fantasy of running my tongue all over his body out of my mind.

'Yes…' Consciousness regained. 'Yes! I wanted to talk to you about work!' I scowled.

'Oh no, no, no, no, no!' said Colette as she entered the kitchen. 'You know my rule, Roxy. No talking about work stuff at home. Save it for the office.'

'But—'

'No buts.…I'm relaxed about a lot of things but not about that. Mixing business with pleasure is always a bad thing. *Always.* Work is for the office. Relaxation and fun is for home.'

'Fine!' I huffed as I threw the yogurt carton in the bin. 'We'll speak when you get in, then.'

I stormed out of the kitchen. Good thing I'd decided to get an early start, as clearly if I relied on Finn or Colette, nothing would ever get done.

~

It felt like I'd barely been at my desk for five minutes before I saw Finn walking through the door an hour later, looking annoyingly hot in another crisp white open-neck shirt, with his dark trousers, which fitted perfectly. I'd just made myself a cup of coffee. No point sitting back down, I wanted to have it out with him now. Get it out of the way.

'Finn. Meeting room. Now, please,' I said, marching off. My blood was boiling like a kettle. I was *so* angry with him, but a lot of the team were already here, including Colette, and I didn't want the office and his precious mother seeing me lose my shit with him. At least in the boardroom, I could let rip in private.

I knew it was Colette who'd ordered him to leave early, but he knew how important the work was that I'd given him, so he could have said no. Finn wasn't like me. He didn't owe her anything, so he could afford to refuse Colette's demands. Or, seeing as he loved using his phone so much, he could have taken some of it to work on in the car on the way to wherever they'd swanned off to.

I turned around to make sure Finn was following me. He was only a few feet behind. *Hold on?* Was he just checking out my arse? *Interesting.* This short burgundy leather skirt was one of my favourites, and it did cling in all the right places…

For God's sake, Roxy. Now is not the time.

I opened the meeting room door.

'Sit down, please.'

'Of course,' he said, walking in, then pulling out a chair for me.

'What are you doing? This isn't a bloody dinner date.'

'Okay, sorry!' He raised his eyebrows. 'Just a habit.'

'I'll stand, thank you very much!' I snapped.

'Anyway, what's up?' he said calmly.

'*What's up?* Are you seriously asking me *what's up?* I'll tell you what's up! You sat at that desk for six hours yesterday and did fuc—' *No, no. I mustn't swear. Must be professional…* 'And you didn't do *anything* that I asked you to, and then you swanned off early with your mum, when you knew how much shi—I mean *stuff* we have to do!'

Gosh. These past few months I'd developed such a potty mouth. Sometimes I just couldn't stop swearing. When I was with Steve, particularly when I was planning to leave him, I used to get so angry and swear constantly in my head. For so long, I had lost my voice and was always too scared to say how I felt. Now that I had the confidence to speak my mind—well, admittedly not to Colette, but to most people—my mouth was like a leaking profanity tap that I couldn't seem to turn off.

'What do you mean I didn't do anything?' He frowned.

'Well'—I folded my arms—'did you call Tony to give him the green light to print the brochures and confirm the quantity?'

'No, but—'

'And did you do any social media posts like I asked you to?'

'I didn't, but—'

'No buts!' I shouted. 'You don't get it. How am I supposed to focus on what I need to do if you can't even do basic things?'

He sighed, stood up, walked towards me and pulled out a chair again.

'Roxanne. You're stressed. Have a seat, please.' he said softly. I don't know why, but I found myself doing as he'd asked. He sat back down in his seat, pulled himself closer to me and stared me straight in the eyes. 'Look, I know you don't know me. As far as you're concerned, I'm the boss's entitled son who's here just to pass the time whilst he's in London, but I assure you that's not the case. If you'd just asked me calmly for an update rather than screaming at me and assuming the worst, then I would have told you that, no, I hadn't called Tony. That's because he was out of the office, so I was *texting* him throughout the day instead. I emailed him first thing in the morning to find out lead times, because when I checked through the brochure that you told me to send straight to print, I found three errors, so rather than disturb you, I emailed the designer to find out how long it would take to correct them, then liaised with Tony to check there was still time to get everything printed. He assured me that as long as I gave him the new artwork and the green light by the end of today, there'd still be time.'

'*Oh*.' I winced. I was sure that I'd checked that document a million times, and I hadn't spotted any typos. Could you imagine if we printed thousands of copies and there were errors? Thank God he'd found them.

'And as for social media, I spent the morning researching our competitors' feeds and seeing what types of imagery they post. Some of them have tacky pictures of half-naked women, which definitely isn't the route we want to pursue. Before you start posting on social media, it's important to have a clear strategy. We need imagery and strong content, so I spent a couple of hours brainstorming and drafting some ideas, which I'm happy to show you if you have time? I'll start rolling out the posts from tomorrow. I'm just waiting for the designer to put some logos on some images. I could probably do it myself, but I'd rather focus on the other high priority tasks you've given me.'

Double oh…

So he *had* been working. *My bad.* Now I looked like a right idiot.

'Right, I see,' I mumbled. 'Sorry, Finn. I—'

'Don't worry about it. Just another misunderstanding right?' he said, resting his hand on mine. It was so big, warm and soft. I felt like he'd just given me an electric shock.

What I am doing? I can't let him touch my hand. It did feel nice, though…

No, no, no! It's not appropriate.

'Yes,' I said, pulling my hand away and breaking eye contact. 'That's right. Just a misunderstanding. I think we'd both better get back to work.'

'Of course,' he said, running his hand through his gorgeous hair and flexing a bicep in the process. 'And I'll be working late tonight, to catch up for yesterday afternoon, when we had to leave early to visit my grandma in hospital.'

'Your—your gran was in the hospital?'

'Yeah, she had a fall at the home and Mum was really worried. She's ninety-one, so she's very fragile. She lives in Liverpool, so we had to leave early to get there before visiting hours ended, and it was a long drive home. That's why we were back so late.'

Shit. There I was slagging him off and he'd gone to see his sick grandmother. I felt terrible.

'Oh my God, Finn.' I winced. 'I didn't realise. How is she? Is she okay?'

'Yeah, she's tough as old boots, that one. By the time we left, she was laughing and joking and saying we weren't going to get rid of her that easily. Mum even joked that she'd done it deliberately just to get me to come up and see her.'

'She wouldn't, would she?' I smiled.

'Nah! Then again, she's a feisty one, so I wouldn't put anything past her. She's amazing. You'd like her. She's a strong, confident woman. Like you...' Our eyes locked, and I felt the electricity again.

'Oh...right...okay,' I stuttered. I wasn't sure what to say. 'Well, I really hope she gets better.'

'I'm sure she'll be fine. They've been taking good care of her there. I'll give her a call later to check on her, though. Just in case.'

As I followed Finn out of the boardroom, I started to think that maybe I'd got him all wrong. If I had, that was good news on the work front, because it meant that maybe he *was* the right person to get stuff done. But in terms of being able to focus and stay out of trouble, it was bad, because if Finn was smart, confident and a good guy on top of being smoking hot, then I had a feeling that I might get myself into a situation that could become very messy. Very messy indeed...

≈

'Done,' said Finn.

'What?' I replied, glancing up from my computer screen to look at him. 'You've finished everything on the list already?' I said.

'Yep!'

'*No way.*'

'Yes *way*! Here,' he said, jumping up and coming over to my desk. He stood behind my chair and leant over my shoulder as he grabbed my mouse. Finn was so close to me I could feel his heart beating and feel his sweet breath on my neck. Even though it was gone 8 p.m. and he'd been at the office for almost twelve hours, somehow he still smelt so good. All musky, manly and fresh at the same time. 'See?' he said, clicking into a Word document on the server. 'All done. Here's the signed confirmation form from the printer. And here's the Twitter, Instagram and Facebook posts for the next two weeks. We'll still need some reactive ones and to do some stories and posts at the show and afterwards, but this will get us started.'

'Oh my God. Thank you! You're a lifesaver. I just wouldn't have had the time do all this myself.'

As much as I hated to admit it, Colette was right. Finn did seem to have a lot of marketing experience. He couldn't have learnt all of this just from working here for a few summers when he was a kid. I wondered what his story was.

'You really need an agency to manage all this for you,' he said, pulling up a chair beside me.

'Tell me about it! Once the show is over, I need to do some research to find someone who can take all this PR and social media stuff off my hands.'

'I agree. So, seeing as we've had a productive day all round, what do you say we go for a drink to have a mini-celebration?'

'Um, well…'

He was staring at me again with those hypnotic eyes. A drink with Finn was *not* a good idea. I was finding it hard to control myself around him when I was sober. Once a few drops of alcohol passed my lips, all my inhibitions would go straight out the window and I'd end up jumping him. I knew I would.

'Thanks, but I've still got a few things to finish up here. You go home. You've worked really hard today. I'll see you in the morning.'

'Are you sure I can't tempt you?'

Yes, you bloody can, Finn. That's the problem. Colette was cool about most things, but I got the feeling she wouldn't be happy with me getting involved with her son. I mean, she didn't even like me *talking* about work at home, for goodness' sake.

'It's better if I don't…' I said, focusing on the screen in front of me.

'Fair enough,' he said, standing up and resting his hand gently on my shoulder. 'Another time, maybe?'

'Yeah, maybe,' I replied as he slowly moved his hand from my shoulder and down the middle of my back. *Oh my God. His touch…*

'Goodnight, Roxy.'

'Goodnight, Finn.'

Holy shit.

Something told me that the longer Finn was around, the harder he was going to be to resist…

CHAPTER FIVE

Finally home.

I glanced at my watch. 10.59 p.m. I was leaving the office later and later. I should have packed up after eight like Finn did, but I told myself I'd just respond to a few more emails, then before I knew it, it had gone 10 p.m.

I unzipped my boots, hung my coat on the stand, then gently put my bright yellow handbag down in the hallway. I'd got it from Colette. Some fancy French or Italian designer brand I couldn't pronounce and knew I couldn't afford. Donald had bought it for her, but she'd said it was too *loud*, so she was going to take it to the charity shop. Luckily I'd managed to catch her before she left and asked if I could have it instead. "Of course, darling," she'd said. And so it became mine. Went lovely with my black leather skirt. In fact, it was perfect for brightening up any outfit. Definitely one of my faves.

Anyway, I needed to eat. I was starving but couldn't be arsed to make anything that took more than a few seconds to prepare. Just as I walked into the kitchen, weighing up whether to have beans on toast or cereal, I spotted a Post-it note on the oven door. I peeled it off to take a closer look.

I made dinner. Chicken curry. Saved you some so you wouldn't have to cook when you got home. It's in the fridge. Enjoy!
Finn x

He made dinner? *For me?* I felt my heart flutter. *That's so sweet.*

I opened the fridge, and sure enough, there was a plate with a cover on it and another note:

All you have to do is warm it up in the microwave.
I've set it for two minutes.
Fork, glass, bottle of wine and napkin already on the table.
Finn x

I glanced at the microwave, which was indeed set for two minutes, then looked over at the kitchen table to see everything neatly laid out for me, along with a single red rose in a slim vase.

Oh...

That was actually really cute. Romantic, even. I was definitely *not* expecting all that. I'm not normally one to get taken in with soppy stuff, but for Finn to do something for me meant a lot. In the eleven years that we were married, Steve never even made me a slice of toast.

Finn was chipping away at my heart. I could feel it thawing. Not going all *hearts and flowers I want to get married and have his babies* thawing. Just, you know… tenderising it. Ever so slightly.

Dammit.

I poured myself a glass of wine and took a large gulp. Very nice. This wasn't one of Colette's bottles. She only ever drank Malbec or Pinot Noir, and this was a Merlot. He must have bought it specially. *This man…*

I popped the plate in the microwave, and just as I pressed start, I heard the front door close. Must be Colette. She always got home around this time after going out with Donald.

Actually, there was no name on the Post-it note. What if the food wasn't for me, and Finn had made it for his mum? No, no. He'd know she always went out for dinner. Pretty sure it was for me.

For some reason, I found myself whipping the rose out of the vase and shoving it, along with the Post-it, note underneath a newspaper that was left on the kitchen counter from this morning. *Silly, really*. It was just a flower and an innocent note. Colette would understand Finn was just being nice. Wouldn't she?

'Hello, Roxy. Having a late-night snack?' said Colette as she walked into the kitchen and put the kettle on.

'Dinner, actually. I was working late at the office.'

'Oh, right, I see. Great!'

Colette really was strange sometimes. On the one hand, she was really kind helping me get back on my feet, but on the other, she seemed completely oblivious to the fact that I wasn't paid to work at the office so late. She must have realised I went above and beyond the call of duty, yet she never showed any sign of appreciation. Maybe she saw the overtime as payback for the extra things she footed the bill for, like me seeing her therapist.

'How was your dinner with Donald?'

'Lovely, thanks. Actually, he mentioned that Terrence had called you yesterday and left a message, but you hadn't replied?'

Cringe. I'd already replied to his text on Sunday to say I didn't think it was a good idea for us to see each other again.

'I told him over the weekend that I wasn't interested, so I'm not sure why he—'

'I think you should definitely see him again,' she interrupted. 'He really enjoyed his evening with you, and I think he's exactly what you need, Roxy. A very successful, nice, stable man. Maybe we should all go out to dinner together? That would be wonderful!'

Sometimes I felt like I was talking to a brick wall.

'I don't think he's my type, to be honest, Colette, and I've got so much on with the show…'

'Well, after the show, then. Don't worry. I'll set something up. Anyway, there haven't been any guests here tonight, have there, Roxy?'

'Guests?' I frowned.

'Yes,' she said, tossing a peppermint teabag into a mug. 'Female guests. *Women.*'

What is she on about?

'Not that I know of. But like I said, I was working late, so I've only just got home. Why? Were you expecting someone?' I checked the food in the microwave and put it on for another minute, just in case.

'That's a relief,' she sighed. 'No. Well, *yes*. It's just that now Finn's back, I'm worried about some unsavoury women crawling out of the woodwork and distracting him. As much as I'm looking forward to lots of grandchildren in the future, Finn needs to focus on his career right now, not get involved with any floozies. God knows what they'd do to wrap him around their filthy little fingers. Especially that Ruth girl,' she scowled, pouring hot water into her mug.

'Ruth?'

'His good-for-nothing ex. It would be just her style to try and sneak in whilst I'm not here and lead my boy astray. And then there's that Clarissa girl. *Ugh*.' She shuddered. 'Well, I say *girl*. She was a grown woman. A temp I had filling in for Raquel years ago whilst she was on annual leave. Finn was working there during the holidays and she was constantly flirting and making eyes at him. *So unprofessional*. Finn was barely twenty-three at the time and she was several years older. One afternoon I caught her with her hand on his shoulder, perching on his desk. Shameless cougar, preying on Finn. Trying to get her filthy claws into my son. Well, there was no way I was having that. I called the agency straight away to tell them her services were no longer required and made sure she never came back. Can you believe she asked me for a reference for another job? The cheek of it! If I had my way, she'd never work in the industry again.'

Seriously? Was she saying she fired a temp just for touching Finn's shoulder? That was ridiculous. And surely illegal. Although, Colette was too smart to have given that as a reason. She would have made something else up.

Not only that, what was with the age comment? Donald was several years older than her, and she's always banging on about the benefits of me dating pensioners, so why did she seem to have a problem with this Clarissa woman being a few years older than Finn? Talk about sexist double standards. And anyway, at twenty-three, Finn was still a grown man, so what did it matter to her?

'But like you said, that was years ago. Finn's an adult. I mean he must be what? Approaching his thirties? So surely he can decide who he dates or what guests he invites home whilst he's here.'

'He's only just turned twenty-seven. Still very young and impressionable. And no. He's far too kind and sweet to realise that these women are trying to dig their claws in and manipulate him. I'm his mother and it's my job to protect him from them. Finn's got a bright future ahead of him. I've spent years nurturing him, sending him to the best schools, the best college, the best university, supporting him whilst he did a string of unpaid internships to build up his experience. His father helped in his own way too, of course, when he moved to LA. But Finn is my only son, and if anyone tries to harm him in any way or do *anything* which will distract or stop him from fulfilling his potential, I will make their life hell.'

Wow.

Her scowl and the look of anger in her eyes said Colette meant every word. I'd never seen her look so serious before. Colette was normally so breezy and light-hearted about things.

I'd known she would frown on a relationship in the

office, particularly if it involved Finn, and I'd known she would be overprotective, but I hadn't thought she'd be *that* extreme. *Damn*.

'Well, like I said, I don't think anyone's come to the house, but I've been here all of ten minutes, so I can't be sure.'

'*Good*. Well, keep an eye out for me. As you know, I'm often out late with Donald, and I don't want any of those hussies hanging around. Finn tends to attract a lot of female attention wherever he goes, so I need to be on high alert at all times. I'm already keeping a close eye on that new girl at the office, *Jodie*, who I've noticed has been fluttering her eyelashes a little too much when he's around. These women have no shame. Anyway, I best get to bed. I'll leave you to your dinner. Goodnight.'

'Goodnight, Colette.'

I took the plate out of the microwave and sat down. *Jeez*. That was intense. In a way, it was a good thing that we'd had that conversation. It gave me clarity. It was a reminder of why I needed to nip any attraction towards Finn firmly in the bud. Like Colette said, work stuff was for the office and personal stuff was for home. Yes, it was difficult because Finn and I were effectively living *and* working together, but his reason for being here was to assist me. At work. That was where our relationship needed to begin and end.

I devoured the food in a flash. It was bloody delicious and definitely a million times better than beans on toast or cereal. I was even tempted to lick the plate. I couldn't believe Finn made that. Given how pampered he must have been by his mum and probably his dad too, I'd had him down as more of a microwave meal or takeaway kind of guy.

Maybe he'd ordered it in and then just put it on the plate. Or used one of those ready-made sauce jars? I walked over and opened the bin. Nope. All I could see was an empty pack of chicken and some vegetable shavings. Not a jar or any restaurant containers in sight. *Impressive.*

Just as I turned around to go and sit back down, in walked Finn. Topless.

Holy shit.

All he was wearing was a pair of tight black boxer shorts, which left nothing to the imagination, and I mean *nothing*. And that display he was rocking down there was setting off my imagination: *big time*. It looked like an anaconda had escaped from a South American tropical forest and climbed straight into his pants.

Sweet Jesus.

Surely that couldn't be real. *He must have stuffed a pairs of socks down there*, I thought as I sat down and desperately tried to stop myself from staring.

'Oh, hi, Roxy,' he said casually. 'Didn't hear you come in. Just came down to get some milk.' He turned to face the fridge, which gave me a delicious view of his arse in the process.

Mmm.

Normally I hate when people drink milk straight from the bottle rather than pouring it into a glass. Ridley at work did it all the time. But right now, I didn't care. All I could see was Finn's bulging muscles as he flexed his arm to tip it back into his mouth. And of course the side profile of the other bulge as he slowly turned to face me.

Shit.

I hope he hasn't seen me looking. What am I even saying? That's the least of my worries. The conversation I'd just had with Colette a few minutes ago told me all I needed to know about the dangers of having these kinds of thoughts about her son.

'So what do you think?' he said.

Of your body? Ten out of ten.

Oops. Just realised, he was looking over at the empty plate. Where were my manners? I'd been so fixated on admiring his physique, I'd forgotten to say thank you. Clearly I'd conveniently forgotten about keeping things professional too…

'That curry was bloody amazing! Thanks. You didn't have to go to all that trouble.'

'Well,' he said, running his hands through his thick hair and flexing a bicep again in the process, 'I know you've been working really hard and the last thing you'd feel like doing when you got home is cooking, so, you know…' He shrugged his shoulders and approached the table. 'Glad you liked it.'

'I really did.'

He was now literally standing literally two feet in front of me. And as I was sitting down, his package was right in my eye line, which was *very* distracting.

Focus…

'Did you see your mum?' I blurted out. 'She was asking about you a minute ago.'

I looked upwards. *Nope. That's no better.* Now his magnificent chest was in my view. It looked *so* solid.

'Yeah, briefly, but she was tired.'

'Good. Great!' I said, still desperately trying not to stare. Never mind a six-pack. That was more like an *eight-*

pack he was rocking. Or ten? Was that a thing? Given the chance, I'd happily volunteer to run my hands over each one individually to count. Y'know, just to double-check my maths was correct…

No, no, no!

I needed to leave before I did something crazy, like try to stroke his leg. *Or worse…*

'I, er…I've got to go and…and…' *Think, Roxy, think*. I jumped up. 'I better go and take a shower. I'll wash up my plate afterwards…' I picked up the newspaper with the Post-it note and rose underneath, then edged backwards out of the kitchen door, bashing my leg on the counter in the process. *Ouch*. 'Thanks again for dinner. Much appreciated. Cheers!'

Cheers?

That sounded *so* cheesy.

I raced up the stairs, closed my bedroom door and slid down on the floor. This was silly. *Ridiculous. I see a half-naked man and I turn to jelly.* There were plenty of guys out there that I could go for, who weren't the boss's son, so I needed to put a stop to these stupid thoughts racing around in my head. *Right now.*

No more fantasising. No more ogling.

I would block all thoughts of Finn from my mind, look for other men and concentrate on the show.

It was for the best.

Definitely the safest and most sensible option all round.

CHAPTER SIX

'Sorted,' said Finn, leaning back in his chair.

'What is?' I asked.

'The competition. We'll be giving away a bundle of products worth a grand to one lucky person who visits our stand and enters the prize draw during the show. I've been emailing your cousin Alex, and she's arranged for it to be promoted on the exhibition's website. We'll get the editor of their affiliated mag to come and draw the winner with Mum on the last day, which will be a brilliant photo op and give the company some great exposure after the show.'

'Wow.' I smiled. 'That's *amazing*! You're not just a pretty face, are you?'

'So you think I'm pretty, do you?' He grinned.

Why the bloody hell did I say that? Where is my filter when I need it? Oh, that's right: I don't seem to have one.

'It's just a saying, Finn,' I replied confidently, managing to rescue myself. 'It's not like I said I wanted to jump your bones or anything.'

Foot in mouth once again. Someone drag me out of this hole I'm digging before HR collars me.

'That's a shame…' Finn smirked.

Really? So he'd be up for it?

No, no, no! What am I thinking? I know I said I'd like a younger man, but I meant five or six years younger. Ten years tops. Not a twenty-seven-year-old. When he was born, I was only a couple of years away from leaving secondary school. Did Colette have a point? Would it just be wrong?

In any case, there was no way. I could not—I repeat, *could not*—go there.

'Anyway,' I said, pulling myself back to reality, 'well done, good job and all that.' I jumped up from my desk and started walking swiftly to the office kitchen. 'I've got to go and do a…a *thing*. Back in a minute…'

A *thing?*

Bloody Nora. This was bad. *Really bad.*

I stood with my back against the wall beside the water cooler and closed my eyes. Even though I knew I shouldn't, I was starting to like him. I could *feel* it. It was because of what happened last night. I'd been having flashbacks about him all morning. *Correction.* I hadn't been able to get him out of mind ever since I'd run off to my room. Which was probably why I made that stupid comment about jumping his bones earlier, because it was *exactly* what I wanted to do.

Sounds nuts, but it was like my libido had been injected with gallons of coffee and Red Bull. It was woken up. *Big time*. And now it was refusing to go back to sleep.

I hadn't felt like this for ages. After I'd left Steve and for months after that, I was a mess. My focus was on putting one foot in front of the other and getting my life back together. The last thing I was thinking about was sex. Especially after having such awful experiences during my marriage.

I hated sex with my ex. When he used to climb on top of me, I used to think, *just let me sleep*. But I'd always go along with it, because I wanted to be a good wife. Everything from start to finish was horrible. The way he'd just enter me without even trying to get me in the mood, the heaviness of his body. Being covered in his sweat. *God, he used to sweat like a pig.* The sheets were always soaked through. Sometimes the sticky, smelly drops would fall from his face into my mouth and my eyes. *Gross.* I tried keeping them closed once, but he demanded that I look at him. And then when it was over, I'd have to lie there in the damp bed as he'd go straight to sleep and changing the bedding would disturb him, plus he insisted I stay where he could see me all night. I couldn't wait to jump in the shower the next morning.

That was why I was so surprised at how my body had reacted when Finn had come back from his run that morning and how, given half the chance, I would have happily licked his sexy, sweaty chest faster than you could say *perspiration*. I just didn't know what had come over me. I couldn't get my head around what Finn was doing to me. The effect he was having on me.

When I'd realised a couple of months ago that I was starting to get the urge again, I'd invested in a few toys to tide me over and had read some books on dating and sex after a divorce to help get my mind back in the game, ready for when I started trying to put myself out there again. So things were okay. The libido situation was all under control. Even after that thing with Terrence, I was still feeling calm. But ever since Finn had arrived on the scene, it was like I'd become a raving nympho.

As much as I knew it was wrong on so many levels, instead of focusing on this exhibition like I'd told myself I would do last night, all I'd been thinking about was what would have happened if I'd pulled Finn into me and peeled those boxer shorts down his big, muscular thighs.

Oh my God.

That was what I was dreaming about in the shower and again when I was in bed. Imagining what it would be like to feel him on top of me. To feel Finn inside me. I couldn't sleep. I needed to release. And I didn't even need to use my vibrator. Just thinking about him made me come. *Twice.*

It was happening. Picturing his face and his hot body was making me tingle all over again…

Fuck.

Colette's words swirled around in my mind.

"If anyone tries to do anything which will stop him from fulfilling his potential, I will make their life hell."

Technically, hooking up with Finn wouldn't *stop him from fulfilling his potential*, would it? It could just be an innocent fling. *Just sex. That's all.* I wouldn't be looking to 'trap' him or stop him from building his career, so what would be the harm?

"I will make their life hell."

No.

I could look at it from a million different angles, but deep down I knew full well that Colette would *not* think it was okay. And if she was horrified at an age gap of a few years with that temp, God only knows what she'd say about a fourteen-year difference…

What was that saying? *If in doubt, leave it out.*

Best to avoid the risk.

Yep.

As sweet as my Finn fantasies were, somehow, I needed to stop. *And I really mean it this time.*

I needed to get Finn out of my mind *now*. Otherwise I was in danger of doing something that would put my job, the roof over my head, my relationship with Colette and the stability and freedom I had worked so hard to achieve in major jeopardy.

CHAPTER SEVEN

What a day. It was a productive one, though. We'd got so much done that I was finally starting to feel like this exhibition wasn't going to be a complete disaster. I had Finn to thank for a lot of that.

I'd tried not to gush too much. It wasn't my style, and if I was going to stand any chance of resisting temptation, I also needed to make sure he didn't notice that I fancied him, as if he realised it was remotely mutual, it might be like waving a red flag to a bull, and my willpower was already feeling about as strong as a bowl of jelly.

Even though I'd spent ages rebuilding my confidence, Finn made me nervous. It wasn't that he did anything bad to make me feel uncomfortable. It was just his presence. The way he looked was enough to make me tongue-tied, which was embarrassing. But it was more than that. It was also how he carried himself. He knew that people just saw him as 'the boss's son', but that didn't faze him. He just put his head down and got on with it. He was smart and genuine. And really kind, which was really attractive. So sexy. *Oh God.* See what I mean? Just thinking about him made me go all funny and out of control. I wasn't used to all this stuff.

I wanted to be able to shake off these feelings and ignore him, but I couldn't, and it was really annoying because this wasn't part of my plan at all. My plan was to get this show out of the way, start having more of a social life, try out the dating apps, go on dates with a load of hot guys and hopefully have lots of no-strings-attached safe sex along the way to get me properly back on the horse, as that Terrence encounter didn't really count. Getting all mushy over some man that, give or take a few years, might be young enough to be my son and putting myself on Colette's hit list was definitely *not* on the agenda.

'So that's me done for the day,' said Finn as he stood beside my chair. I'd been so lost in my thoughts, I hadn't even noticed that he'd got up from his desk. 'Unless there's anything else you want me to do?'

He's talking about work, Roxy. Not personal services. Get your mind out of the gutter.

'Um, erm, no,' I said, turning my chair to face him. 'That's fine, Finn. You can go. We've ticked a lot off our to-do list today. Thanks again.' He looked me in the eyes and didn't say a word. It felt like he'd drawn me into some kind of hypnotic state and somehow I'd lost the ability to speak or move.

Bollocks. I was getting drawn in again. I didn't know how much time had passed, but it had definitely been a long silence. What was going to happen next? It felt like one of those moments that I'd seen on romcoms where he'd move closer, kneel down, take my face into my hands and start snogging my face off. I tell you what, I'd definitely pay good money to have his lips all over me. Not that I'd ever thought about paying for sex, but y'know, *just saying…*

Damn.

How many times? How many times do I need to remind myself that this cannot happen?

'Anyway…' I spun my chair back around to face my computer to try and break his spell, but as I did, Finn grabbed the back of it and spun it back around again to face him. 'What are you doing?' I frowned.

'Roxy,' he said softly. 'Shall we go somewhere? Away from the office? Away from home? For a drink? For dinner? To be by ourselves? *Alone?*'

I'd love nothing more, but…

Willpower, hang on in there. *Please. Note to self: I must ensure Finn and I are never left in the office or anywhere alone ever again.*

'Why? We *are* alone,' I said innocently. 'Everyone has gone home.'

'*Come on.*' He raised his eyebrows. 'You know *why…*' He moved closer. He was now literally standing an inch away from me.

Hold it together, Rox. Hold it together.

God, he smells so good. Temptation is a bitch.

'Sorry, I don't,' I replied. I mean, I *thought* I knew what he was getting at, but I couldn't be totally sure.

Yeah, I'd caught him checking out my arse a few times, staring at me for longer than he should, and of course there was the making dinner and conveniently strolling downstairs half-naked with his crown jewels practically bursting out of his boxers, but even though they seemed like pretty obvious signs, I was still new to this stuff. I hadn't flirted with guys for donkey's years. And Finn was a millennial. Didn't they all use apps, messages and emojis to share feelings these days? All the books I'd read were about dating after a divorce or in your thirties and forties, so I didn't have the lowdown on how these twenty-somethings rolled.

And who was to say it wasn't a trap? Set up by his mum to see if she could trust me? Or worse still, a joke? Maybe his friends had dared him to pull a forty-something woman just to see if he could. To stroke his ego. To show that he'd *got it*.

No. I'm not falling for it. I'm not about to embarrass myself.

'I could be wrong,' he said, edging closer to me, with his leg now brushing against mine, 'but I'm picking up a vibe here. I like you, Roxy, and despite the way you try to hide it, I think you might like me too.'

Busted.

I thought I'd manage to disguise it. *Clearly not.* Seemed I was gawping a lot more than I'd thought.

Well, this is awkward. Even more so as the heat from his leg was sending shockwaves right through me. What the hell was I supposed to do, or say, when my body was telling me to jump straight onto his lap? If it was anyone else, I reckoned I would be all over him like warm butter on toast.

Correction: if it was anyone else that looked like him, but was a few years older, wasn't my boss's son, and if I wasn't in the office, then I totally would. But as it stood, it wasn't, he wasn't, he was and I was, so I couldn't.

I needed to do what I always did when I found myself feeling weak around Finn. Remove myself from the situation. Away from him. But my chair was against my desk and now he'd decided to stand right in front of me, blocking the way.

It's the only solution.

'Look, Finn…' I stood up slowly. My body was now against his and it felt so bloody good. *Shit.* I glanced up at him, knowing I should immediately pull myself away, but somehow not being able to. 'I don't know what you *think* you're feeling or what you believe I think about you, but you're here to do a job. That's all. Pure and simple. The show will be done in just over a week and not long after that you'll be back on a plane to LA and back to your normal life, so let's not make things complicated.' *I'd managed to keep it together. Well done.* 'I need to go to the…to the…'

Dammit. Lost it again. Must be because I can feel something hard pressing against me…

Fuck.

I have got *to get out of here.*

Now.

I pushed past him. Finn reached out for my arm and gently pulled me back.

'Stop…' I said weakly. He looked at me again, his breathing growing faster.

'So are you saying that I'm wrong? That you *aren't* attracted to me? That it's in my imagination? That there's nothing between us? That you can't *feel* the connection? The spark?'

I glanced down at the floor. There was no way I could lie to his face. He'd take one look at me and see the truth straight away.

'Finn,' I sighed. 'You are twenty-bloody-seven. I'm

forty-one! You are Colette's son. Colette is my boss. She took me in. Gave me somewhere to live. A job. A second chance at life. She thinks the sun shines out of your backside. And she trusts me. I couldn't do that to her. It's just not worth the risk.'

'How do you know?' he said, lifting my chin so I could look him in the eyes, then taking my hands in his. 'I may be twenty-seven, but age is just a number. I don't give a shit if you're forty-one. You are smart and confident and fucking hot! You are a *thousand* times more attractive to me than some twenty-one-year-old. And as for my mum, she needs to realise that I'm a man, not the boy in those godawful photos she insists on displaying everywhere. I make my own decisions, including who I choose to date, and if she can't get over that—well, then, she can't be in my life.'

Whoa.

If he was trying to make me think that anything could ever happen between us, then he'd just given me another reason to shut any thoughts of him firmly down. *Right now.*

As if Colette's threats weren't bad enough, Finn had just basically said that he would cut ties with his mum if she wasn't okay with the idea of us hooking up. *Jesus.* Could you imagine? I pitied the woman that ever dared come between Colette and her darling son. Forget just making their life hell. That's a murder scene right there.

No, thanks. As hot as he was, I'd only just got my life back, and I wasn't going to lose it for a few minutes of pleasure. *Forget it.*

'Finn,' I said, releasing my hands. 'You're a great guy. You're doing a good job helping out here. Let's just leave it at that. Go home, take a cold shower and forget about this conversation because you and me hooking up, or doing *anything* together, just won't work. It's never going to happen.'

Finn walked calmly over to his desk and picked up his coat. *At least he's got the message. Phew.* That was a close call.

'Okay,' he said, standing in front of me again. 'I get it. You're trying to do the right thing. But you see, that only makes me like you more. As I said earlier, I may be twenty-seven, but I've lived enough to know that sometimes feelings become too strong to be denied. Despite our best intentions and all our attempts to be honourable, sometimes, we just have to admit that at the end of the day, we're only human and sometimes we can't fight these things.' He took a step closer. His lips were now almost touching mine. *Shit.* 'And most of all, what I've learnt during almost three decades on this earth is that in life, even if you *think* you're in control of a situation and plan to stay strong and resist temptation, you should absolutely *never* say *never*, because you just *never* know, Roxy, what might happen next...'

CHAPTER EIGHT

That's the thing with working in an office. When you're busy, it's so easy to sit at your desk for hours without moving. Apart from going to the loo, sometimes I could go the whole day without getting up. It was really bad. Especially as with all these early starts and late nights, I hadn't had time to go to the gym for ages. Not exactly an ideal recipe for keeping in shape.

Well, no more. Even though the show was now just eight days away, I'd decided that rather than asking one of the girls to grab a chicken salad sandwich for me and then eating it whilst I was working, today I'd walk to the bakery and get it myself. It would only take ten minutes there and back, which was still much less than the hour lunch break I was entitled to, but every little bit helped, and I had a meeting this afternoon, so I couldn't afford to go out for any longer than that. *Yes.* A short time out would mean I could get some air and exercise and still be fresh for my meeting later.

Good plan.

'Just going to grab some lunch, Finn,' I said as I put my computer to sleep. 'Back in ten. Want anything?'

'*Look at you!* Getting up from your desk and venturing into the outside world during working hours!' he quipped. 'Talk about living life on the edge. *Go, Roxy!*'

'Ha-ha. Very funny.' I rolled my eyes. 'So was that a yes or a no to getting you something whilst I'm out?'

'I'm good, thanks. I'll pop out later. As I keep telling you, it's important to step away from your computer for at least half an hour. It's not good for your health sitting down all day.'

'Yes, yes, Granddad. Enough of the lecture,' I said, secretly thinking how sweet it was that he cared. 'Well, if you're sure you don't want anything—'

'Oooh!' shrieked Colette's voice from behind me. 'Did I hear you say you're popping out, Roxy?'

'Yes, but only to—'

'Wonderful!' she beamed. 'Would you be a darling and pick up a gift for Donald for me? He's going away for the whole weekend, so I thought it would be nice to give him a little prezzie when I see him tonight to keep me in his mind.'

For God's sake. Who gets someone a gift just because they're going away for a whole two days?

'The thing is, Colette, I'm only walking to the local bakery around the corner as I've got an important new business meeting this afternoon—'

'Ah, I know, darling, but don't worry. It'll be fine. Just jump in the car quickly and head into town. It won't take long. I'd go myself but you know…seeing as you're going out anyway, it makes sense if *you* go.'

She'd *never* go herself. Apart from doing the weekly

food shop, she hardly ever ran any of her own errands. I was beginning to wonder if that was why she helped me out in the first place. So that she could have someone on call, literally twenty-four seven, to run around after her. *No. Mustn't be ungrateful.* Two years ago, if someone had offered me a chance to be free from Steve and be given a great job, a nice place to live, a car and a new life in exchange for running a few errands, I would have bitten their hand off. So now that I had all of that and more, I couldn't complain. In the grand scheme of things, picking up a gift wasn't a big deal.

'Okay,' I replied. 'What do you need me to get for you, Colette?'

'Whatever you think he'll like will be fine. You'll figure it out. Better run. Just give it to Raquel once you've bought it. Thanks, darling!'

What? Raquel's here today? Why can't she send her? And how the hell am I supposed to know what Donald will like? I didn't even know him. Now I was going to have to drive to the high street, which completely defeated the object of getting away from my desk. I didn't want to go for a drive. I snatched up my car keys and my handbag.

'You can say no, you know…' said Finn, sensing my frustration. 'If you've got too much on?'

'No, it's *fine*,' I huffed. 'My meeting isn't until 3 p.m., so if I leave now, I should be back by 1.30 p.m., which will give me enough time. Thanks.'

I approached the high street, scanning left and right for a parking space. Damn.

I couldn't find any spaces anywhere. I continued driving further and further down the street.

Finally! I found a spot right at the end, pulled into it quickly, called the automated number to pay the parking fee with my card and then set off.

I wracked my brain trying to work out what to get and then decided that aftershave would probably be easiest.

After walking for at least ten minutes, I eventually reached the department store. Why was there a queue at the perfume counter? This was exactly what I *didn't* need. I'd only put half an hour on the parking meter. And now there was no phone reception in the store to call and top it up. If I left to go outside, I'd lose my place in the queue.

When I eventually got served I'd just grab an expensive aftershave. I reckoned that was what all loaded people like Donald cared about. Having fancy stuff to display in their bathroom. He probably already had thousands of bottles anyway. Maybe he didn't even buy anything off the shelf. I bet it was hand-blended according to his unique scent or some nonsense like that. And I guarantee Colette wouldn't give me the money back for this either. She never did. And knowing that she shelled out hundreds, maybe even thousands on stuff I hadn't paid her for, like those therapy sessions, putting it on expenses seemed wrong somehow. All these costs counted towards reducing my tab, I supposed.

Four minutes. If I ran, I might just make it back in time. These boots weren't made for walking long distances and definitely not for running, but I had to try. It was already nearly one-thirty and I should have been back at the office by now anyway, so I needed to be quick.

I could see the car in the distance. *Thank God.* Just as I

picked up speed, I felt my ankle twist and I went crashing to the floor.

Ouch!

I looked down to see my right knee bleeding and the heel on my boot looking well and truly mangled. *This is all I need.*

I reached into my handbag and grabbed a tissue to try and blot up some of the blood, then slid the boot off my leg.

What do I do now? I had a meeting in just over an hour. How could I take that with just one boot? I wracked my brain, desperately trying to think of where the nearest shoe menders was. Damn. It was all the way at the other end of the high street—where I'd just come from. Maybe if I drove up there, I could pop in quickly and get my heel fixed? Worth a try.

I dragged myself up slowly from the pavement and hobbled back to the car. I was a few minutes over the time, but thank goodness I didn't get a ticket.

It was already 1.37 p.m. Luckily, there was a spot just outside the shoe menders. I should be able to nip in and out quickly. I parked up and went inside.

'Hi! Mega emergency,' I said, placing the boot on the counter. 'My heel just broke and I need it fixed urgently. Can you help me, please?'

'Course we can, love,' said the stocky man behind the till. 'Ivan's just gone to lunch, but he'll be back in an hour, so if you leave it with us, I'll make sure it's the first job he does. That okay, sweetheart?'

'An hour?' Bollocks! There was no way I could wait that long. 'Is there no one else that can do it before then?' I pleaded. 'It's just that I've got a meeting, so I have to get back to the office.'

'Sorry, sweetheart. That's the best that we can do.'

'Or is there anywhere else you can recommend? Somewhere nearby?' I could feel the sweat building on my forehead.

'Sorry, treacle. We're the only one in town.'

Shit. Shit. *Shit!*

'Okay. Thanks anyway,' I said, grabbing my boot and rushing back outside.

Oh no! You have got *to be joking!*

'Excuse me!' I rushed over to the car. 'Please! *Please* don't give me a ticket! Not today of all days. I was literally just two minutes. Not even that! I only popped into the shop to get my heel mended for a few seconds. *Please!*'

The traffic warden continued preparing the ticket, completely ignoring me, and then slapped it gleefully on the car.

Bastard.

Damn you, Colette! This is all your fault. I'd broken my heel, shelled out ninety quid on a bottle of aftershave for your stupid boyfriend, and now I'd probably be another hundred pounds out of pocket to cover this sodding parking ticket. I was going to be stressed for my meeting and would look like a total idiot with one boot. This was a nightmare. How could she think that getting this for Donald was more important than a new business meeting? Where were her priorities? Then again, where were mine? I should have said no. Or tried to. *Aaargh!*

I jumped in the car, fighting back the tears. *Come on, Roxy. Don't get upset. You've been through worse than this. It's going to be okay. You've prepared for the meeting. It will be fine.*

I'll just work later tonight, I thought, composing myself again. *I'll get it all done. I always do.*

It was 2.05 p.m. as I swung the car into my space at the office. Just as I climbed out of the driver's seat, I saw Finn approaching. He was probably off to get lunch.

'Hey! I was wondering where you'd got to!' he smirked.

'Got held up in town,' I replied, hobbling towards the office.

'Shit! What did you do to your knee? And what happened to your boot? Why are you holding it and not wearing it?'

'Fell over and broke my heel, so now I'm going to have to do the meeting barefoot, which is just peachy, isn't it? Oh, and I got a parking ticket, which is the cherry on top.'

'Fuck.' He winced. 'Well, first we need to get your knee seen to…'

'My knee will be fine. Thanks, Finn. But this is an important meeting and I'm going to look like a right plonker with just one boot. Not exactly a great first impression, is it?'

'Do you have any spare shoes in the office, or does anyone else wear the same size as you?'

'Nope, and my feet are tiny. No one else wears a size three. I'm screwed.'

Finn paused, then smiled like he'd just had a brainwave.

'I've got an idea. Go back inside, get ready for your

meeting and don't worry about your boots. I'll be back shortly.'

'Why, what are you going to do?' I frowned.

'No time to discuss!' said Finn, rushing over to the Range Rover. 'I'll be back.' He jumped in and sped away.

Just as I'd finished setting up my stuff in the board-room, my phone buzzed. It was a text from Finn. Gosh. Was that the time already? Felt like only a few minutes had passed, but it was 2.45 p.m.

Finn

Meet me in the car park. Urgent.

I still wasn't sure what Finn had up his sleeve, but even though I'd only known him a few days, I was starting to feel like he was someone I could rely on, so I was open to trusting that his idea would be something helpful.

I walked barefoot into the car park. Seeing as this was how I'd have to take the meeting, I might as well start getting used to it. To avoid them seeing me with no shoes on, I was thinking of telling them that I'd hurt my leg so I couldn't stand up. It was kind of true. Let's just hope none of them decided to look under the table…

I opened the car door and climbed inside.

'Right,' he said, reaching behind him. 'I wasn't sure which ones you'd want, so I just bought four different choices. I reckon these will go best with the skirt you're wearing…' He picked up a pair of red boots from the back seat and handed them to me. I gasped.

'These are my…how did you? How come you…?' I

glanced behind me and saw a selection of my favourite knee-high boots. 'You drove all the way back home to get these for me?'

'Well, yeah.' He shrugged his shoulders. 'I thought about buying a new pair, but then I figured you'd feel more comfortable if they were your own. No big deal.'

Oh, but it is.

That's so sweet of him.

I love wearing long boots. I remember when I was working in my last job, I was wandering down Oxford Street on my lunch break and I spotted a gorgeous pair in the window of a fancy shoe shop and instantly fell in love. They were pricy, though, and it wasn't like I was earning a lot of money, so each day I'd pass them, drool, then drag myself away because I couldn't afford them.

But then one day, I decided to go and try them on. As I slid my tiny feet into the soft leather and glided the zip smoothly up to the top, I knew I had to have them. They fitted like a glove, and the five-inch heels instantly made me feel more confident.

Before I knew it, I had whipped out my credit card and was standing at the counter as the shop assistant rung it up and officially declared that I was now the proud owner of the most beautiful boots ever made. I couldn't have been happier. Whenever I wanted a shot of confidence, I would slip them on and feel ten feet tall.

But then, not long after I married Steve, when I was tidying up the wardrobe, I noticed my boots had disappeared. I always kept them in the original box so that they'd stay pristine, but it wasn't there. I asked Steve if he'd seen or moved them, but he said he didn't know what I was talking about and that maybe I was confused or had left them at my old flat or something. But I knew that I hadn't. I wouldn't have dreamt of leaving them behind.

It drove me mental for months. What had happened to them? How did a box that big suddenly get lost? It was only after asking him again, about a year later, that he casually confessed that he'd thrown them away because he thought they were 'too tarty' and 'inappropriate'. I was so upset. But somehow, and to this day I still don't know how, he convinced me that it was for the best. That because I was a married woman, I wouldn't need them anymore. That people would think I was a bad person if I wore them and that actually he had done me a favour, protected me from the judgment of others by throwing them out. So rather than screaming, I found myself thanking him. How awful is that? That's how good he was at manipulating me.

Once I'd left Steve and started earning, one of the first things I did was to buy myself two new pairs of knee-high skyscraper-heeled boots, including this bold red pair. It was a kind of *Fuck you, Steve. I can wear whatever the hell I want* moment, and it felt so bloody good. I had been building up my collection ever since and now had about eight different pairs in all different colours and styles. I loved wearing them with a skirt, preferably leather, because again, that's what I liked and it had kind of become my signature style.

'Here,' said Finn, taking the right foot of the boots from my hands and unzipping it. 'Let me…' He spread it open so I could slide my foot inside, then rested his hands on either side of my legs as he started to zip them up. *Slowly. Talk about a Cinderella moment.*

I felt like I'd been struck by lightning. I could feel the

heat from his palms. Wow. Look at those big, manly hands. On my legs. I wished they could stroke me. I wished they could travel, further and further up my body. Past my calf, beyond my knees, up my thighs and then…*oh*…

Finn paused midway. I felt my heart stop. Wondering what would happen next. I turned to face him and our eyes locked. *Look at him.* Jesus. He was so handsome. So *sexy*. Our faces were just inches apart and his hands were still resting on my legs. All it would take was one quick movement. One swift action and everything could change.

No one need know. This car had all the windows blacked out, so no one would see.

He continued zipping up my boot, without breaking his gaze.

'Very nice…' he said.

'Thanks,' I said. His hypnotic eyes were drawing me in again. My mind was racing, thinking of all the things I wanted to happen right now. 'They're my favourites,' I said, struggling to breathe.

'I wasn't talking about your boots…'

He released his hand from the zip, and I felt it travelling up towards my thigh.

God, I want him.

Finn started leaning in. *Oh. So. Slowly.*

This is happening. We're going to kiss. And I don't think I have the power to stop it. Dammit.

Just as our lips were millimetres apart, my phone rang.

I jumped back.

What the hell was I doing? What was I thinking? I had a meeting in what? I grabbed my phone to check the time. It was 2.53 p.m. I had a meeting in *seven fucking minutes* and I was sitting in a car about to kiss Finn. *Colette's son.* This was ridiculous!

'Hello, Julie?' I said, coming to my senses. I wedged the phone between my shoulder and my cheek so I could use my hands to put on the other foot of the boot and zip it up. 'Okay, great, I'm coming. Just had to get some paperwork from the car, but I'm coming back inside. Right now.' I ended the call, then opened the door. 'I've got to go Finn. Thank you. For the boots. I really appreciate it.'

'No worries, but before you go…'

'We can't…'

'No, it's not that,' he said, reaching in his pocket. 'It's your knee. You can't leave it like that. Here,' he said as he ripped a small white packet open. 'It's an antiseptic wipe I got from the first aid kit at home. Let me…' He rubbed it gently across the cut. It stung a little, but any pain was quickly overtaken by the tingles that were racing through my body and between my legs. Finn reached into his pocket again, pulled out a square plaster and placed it over the graze. *So sweet.* 'Okay. Done. Didn't want you to get an infection or something. You better go. You'll ace that meeting, Roxy. I know you will. You're amazing.'

'Thanks again, Finn,' I said, climbing out of the car.

Damn. *This man.*

Sexy, smart, kind *and* caring? That was an impossible combination.

An irresistible cocktail that not even the strongest person on earth could resist. But like it or not, even though I didn't rate my chances, for the sake of my future, I was going to have to give it a bloody good try…

CHAPTER NINE

'Well, this is lovely, isn't it? All three of us together. Away from the office, feeling relaxed and enjoying a nice meal. How wonderful!' beamed Colette.

If you asked me, it was bloody awkward. Colette had been reminiscing about the days when Finn was younger. She'd even got out a photo album at one point and started going through old photos, until Finn had wrestled it out of her hands insisting that I didn't need to see them. *Too right.* Then she'd asked if he'd consider extending his trip, but he'd explained that he was starting a new marketing job for some healthy food company or something, so it wouldn't be possible. I must admit, I was a little gutted to know he'd be leaving in just over a week's time. Purely because he'd been doing a good job at work. That was the only reason. *Honest.*

Just as I was wracking my brain trying to think of an excuse to leave the table and wondering whether I needed to wait another ten minutes or if I could do it within the next ten seconds, which would definitely be preferable, Colette's phone rang.

'Hello, darling. How did it go? *Really? Oh dear*. Right. Oooh! Wonderful....Now? But I haven't...? Well, yes, I suppose....*Oooh!* Okay, then! How exciting! Yes! See you shortly!' She ended the call. 'I hope you don't mind, darlings, but that was Donald. His business trip got cancelled, so he's taking me away to Nice for the weekend instead. The car is already outside. I won't even have time to pack, but he said we could go shopping to pick up some new clothes tomorrow. How exciting! You two will be okay on your own, won't you?'

'Well, actually, I was just going to head upstairs to my room and have an early night,' I said.

'Nonsense! It's six o'clock on a Saturday. The evening has barely begun. There's still plenty of food here and I picked up a nice apple pie from M&S with some thick creamy custard, so you two can have that for dessert. Bye, pumpkin,' she said, squeezing Finn's cheeks.

'Mum! *Seriously*. Can you stop!' Finn snapped. Colette ignored him.

'Roxy, please stay and keep Finn company. I'm sure you can find something to watch on the TV. Or maybe play a board game? Finn knows where to find them. I know you'll take good care of him for me.'

Board games? *Seriously?* And *take good care of him*? You'd think I was babysitting a toddler.

Finn started grinding his teeth. I could tell he was annoyed and wanted to say something but was biting his tongue. *Don't bloody blame him.* I'd be pissed off too.

'Right, better fetch my passport and a few essentials,' said Colette as she disappeared upstairs. It only felt like two minutes later when she ran back down. 'Bye, my darlings!' she shouted, rushing through the door clutching a small overnight bag.

Finn and I both sat at the table in silence. Yet more awkwardness.

He started grinding his teeth again.

'That's bad for you, you know,' I said.

'What is?'

'Grinding your teeth.'

'Right now, I couldn't give a fuck,' he snarled.

'Fair enough!' I said, taken aback by his bluntness. Don't know why, considering I dropped the F-bomb so often you'd think I was competing for first place in the National Profanity Awards.

'Sorry, Roxy. I'm sorry. I didn't mean to snap. It's just she drives me up the wall! She treats me like I'm five years old and it's suffocating. That's one of the reasons I left. I just couldn't stay with her anymore. She just wants to control my life and for me to be her *little boy* forever. Because I haven't been back in London for a while, I was hoping she'd changed, but if anything, she's got worse.'

'I reckon she just misses you.'

'I know, I know. I get it. I'm her only child. She means well. That's why I try and stay cool. To keep her happy. But sometimes it's just too much. Too intense. Especially with the photos. That's the main reason why I stopped letting her take any of me once I started college and refuse to send her any new ones. I got sick and tired of her displaying them everywhere and showing them to people. Like tonight. Bringing out those old photo albums, for God's sake. So embarrassing.'

Aha! So *that's* why Colette only had school photos of

him. I'd wondered why there were none of him as an adult. Interesting, as I would have thought that given how much he'd blossomed and with a face and body like that, he'd love to pose and have his hotness displayed at every opportunity. By the sounds of it, Colette's obsessive photo taking when he was a kid had probably put him off being in front of the camera for life.

'Anyway,' he sighed. 'Enough about that.' Finn stood up and started walking towards me. *Oh shit. What's he going to do?* 'How about I put that pie in the oven and get another bottle of wine?'

'Well, actually, like I said to Colette, I was just about to go up to my room and have an early night.'

'*Come on*, Roxy!' He rolled his eyes. 'Now who's acting like a five-year-old? You want to go to bed at six on a Saturday? Live a little! I'm putting dessert in the oven, and then we can share a bottle of wine and get to know each other better. Deal?'

Nope, no way. Absolutely not. I cannot agree to it. I won't.

'Okay…' I said, the words falling from my mouth before I could stop them.

Will I ever learn? I was alone in the house with Finn, the guy I was finding increasingly fuckable by the second, and I had just agreed to add alcohol into the mix. *Jesus.* That was just asking for trouble.

No, no. It will be fine. There was a bottle of water on the table, so if I drank two glasses for every glass of wine, I'd keep myself on the straight and narrow.

Who am I kidding?

Next thing I knew, I was jumping up to check my hair and make-up in the mirror above the fireplace and making sure there was nothing stuck between my teeth. *Er, hello?* I grabbed a load of mints from the bowl in the centre of the large white marble dining table, then, as I heard him coming back, I quickly sat back down, again trying to act natural.

What am I doing? Tarting myself up and freshening my breath *just in case*? Nothing could happen. *Remember?*

'So…' said Finn, pulling up one of the plush white leather dining chairs beside me and then sitting down so close that our legs were touching. 'Tell me more about you, Roxy. What do you like to do? *For fun*. All I've seen you do since I've been here is work. You're very committed and dedicated, which is great. But I'm interested to know more about the *other* side to your personality…' He rested his elbow on the table and looked into my eyes.

Damn. I hate when he does that. It's so hard for me to concentrate.

Fun? *Chance would be a fine thing.* I'd only just learnt how to function again. Up until now my objective was just to get my head in the right place. Build the foundations to allow me to start going out and living life. But I couldn't very well tell him that, could I? It was a bit too deep. Right now, I *didn't* have a social life. I worked, came home, watched TV, occasionally met up with Alex for a drink, but that was it. Embarrassing, really.

'Well, normally I'm a lot more sociable, you know…' I said, thinking of something which sounded interesting. 'Dancing.' It's true. Before Steve, I used to really enjoy it. That was donkey's years ago now. 'Yeah. I like going dancing and also like watching it on TV. *Strictly Come Dancing* is one of my favourite shows.' Should I have admitted that? Someone like Finn was probably going to think that's so cheesy. *Oh well.*

'Ah! *Dancing with the Stars*! That's what it's called in the States. Don't tell anyone, but I have been known to watch an episode or ten of that show. I love seeing the transformation of someone with two left feet into an expert dancer.'

'Yes!' I said a little too excitedly. '*Exactly!* It's brilliant.' *Wow*. I hadn't thought Finn would be into that at all. He was full of surprises.

'I know someone who works in production on the show over here. If you like it that much, I can probably get you a ticket to watch it live?'

'Really?' My eyes widened. *Gosh, I'd love to be part of the audience. That'd be beyond cool.*

'*Sure*. I've been before. Years ago, though. Raj is a good friend of mine, so it shouldn't be a problem to organise. What about you, Roxy? Do you have many friends in the area?'

'Well, I wouldn't say loads, but yeah, a few,' I lied. 'Yeah. Normally I'd be out with my friends and having fun, but this exhibition has taken over my life, so until it finishes next weekend, I'll be chained to my desk.' That part at least was true.

'So you like chains, do you?' He smirked. '*Interesting...*'

'I didn't mean...' I took a large glug of my wine. *Aaaargh!* Why did he always make me so tongue-tied?

'Don't worry,' Finn chuckled. 'I'm familiar with the saying. I'm just pulling your leg. So you like going out with friends and having fun? Do you have any *special* friends right now? Y'know. *Male* friends, or like a *boyfriend*?'

I could lie, couldn't I, and say I was seeing someone? That would stop him from thinking there was any chance of us hooking up.

'Er, no…'

That wasn't what I was supposed to say. Dammit.

'Interesting…' He grinned.

'I mean, *maybe*…' I wasn't supposed to say that either. *For Christ's sake.* How hard was it to just say I was already dating?

'So that's not a definite yes, then?'

'It's not a no either, Finn…' I said, trying to recover.

'Mmm…' He licked his lips and my heart started pounding. *This man*. He reached over and brushed a strand of hair off my face. 'You're gorgeous, Roxy.' He stroked my cheek and it was like the floodgates opened in my knickers. *Jesus*. I pressed my legs together tightly. If I didn't, I was pretty sure they'd flop open and I'd start pleading for him to *take me* like some horny woman in a romance novel. The truth was, I *was* horny and that was *exactly* what I wanted to say. And exactly what I wanted him to do. I wanted Finn inside me. I wanted him to fuck me. *So badly.* But I couldn't.

I. Must. Not. Let. It. Happen.

I jumped up, and his hand fell.

'I'd better clear the plates away,' I said, stacking them on top of each other and rushing out of the dining room.

Just as I was scraping them out into the bin, Finn came into the kitchen. I tried to ignore him and went over to the sink, turned on the taps and started washing up. Finn stood behind me, reached around my waist and turned the taps off. I turned them back on again. He pressed his body into mine and turned them back off. I could feel his sweet breath on my neck and his hard-on pressing on my back.

Oh God. This is so hard. Literally.

'You do realise we have a dishwasher, right?'

He pressed himself harder into me.

This is torture. I took a deep breath, trying to focus on replying instead of wishing he'd just rip my clothes off.

'Yes, but…I…'

Suddenly I felt Finn gently wrap his hands around my waist and it was like my heart stopped. His hands moved upwards and he started stroking my breasts.

Oh fuck.

I should ask him to stop, I said to myself, *before things go any further. I really, really need to ask him to stop…*

The words didn't come out of my mouth. They couldn't. And I was glad, because the truth was that I definitely did *not* want him to stop. I wanted him to carry on doing *exactly* what he was doing. *And a whole lot more…*

Finn's big, warm hands slid underneath my top. As they brushed against my skin, I gasped. I couldn't help it. He unclipped my bra and tossed it to the floor. Then he started circling my rock-hard nipples and began kissing my neck.

Sweet Jesus.

My knickers were soaked through, and now I just wanted him to rip them off and take full advantage.

Shit. This is wrong. *So, so wrong.* Yet it still felt *so* damn right. How the hell was I supposed to resist?

As his hands started heading down to my belly button, I tried to referee the fight that was going on in my head between my libido and my conscience. My mind was telling me that I needed to push him away, but my body was telling common sense to take a long walk off a short bridge. I knew I should be sensible, but...*oh*...*my*...*God*.

I couldn't focus. And I didn't want to. I didn't even want to think. I just wanted to enjoy this moment. Have fun. Let loose. I'd spent so many years doing the right thing. Toeing the line. Doing as I was told. Obeying Steve. Doing everything Colette wanted. Trying to please other people. But what about me? Why couldn't I do something for *me* for a change? Didn't I deserve some happiness? Finn and I were both adults, so why did we need Colette's permission? Why couldn't we just do whatever we wanted? Like Finn said, he wasn't her little boy anymore.

Do you know what?

Fuck it.

No more thinking. No more worrying about Colette. *I'm doing this. For me.*

Just like that, a switch went off in my brain and the last of my inhibitions flew out the window. Decent, honourable Roxy evaporated, and *Rampant Roxy*, my new hungry-for-sex alter ego, took over. And something told me there was no way anyone was going to stop her.

I have a hot twenty-seven-year-old whose hands are all over my body, and I am going to grab the bull by the horns and make the most of it, goddammit.

Finn ground into me as his right hand slid beneath my black leather skirt, then inside my knickers. *Holy shit.* He began stroking my clit. I couldn't breathe. I felt like my whole body was about to shatter.

As his right hand carried on stroking me, his left hand lifted my chin.

'Turn around, please,' he said softly. I spun round to

face him. Our eyes locked and I felt my knees buckle. Finn leant forward and pressed his lips onto mine. The kisses started slowly, but within seconds, we really started going for it. Snogging like we were long-lost lovers who hadn't seen each other for years.

His tongue flicked against mine. I pushed my hands underneath his white T-shirt and began stroking his firm chest. It was like a sculpture. *So damn smooth. So damn fine.* I pulled the T-shirt up and over his head and threw it on the floor. I carried on running my hands all over him, and I felt his heart pounding like a heavy drum and bass beat. I reached into his jeans, and he groaned like a hungry animal.

'Tell me what you want, Roxy,' he panted. 'Don't hold back. Say what you feel. *Tell me.* Anything you want and I'll do it.'

I hadn't been asked that in a long time. In fact, *never*. Sex had always been about pleasing a man. Never about my own pleasure. It was more of a chore. Yeah, I used to dream about what I wanted. Y'know: having sex all around the house. In different rooms. Across the furniture. In different positions. But asking for it? Saying that out loud? *No way.* I was worried I'd be laughed at. Steve would have thought I was a freak or a slut. But right now, I felt like I *could*. Like it would be okay.

Before I had time to give it any more thought, Rampant Roxy took over.

'I want you to take me into the dining room, spread me across that fancy table and fuck me, Finn,' I commanded.

Saying that felt *good*. I looked up at Finn nervously to gauge his reaction.

He didn't say a word.

He just scooped me up into his arms, carried me back into the dining room and laid me down across the cold marble, just like I'd asked. Well, almost…there was still the final part of my request to fulfil…

Finn reached into his wallet, pulled out a condom, unbuckled his jeans, pulled down his boxers, and then stepped out of them.

Jesus Christ.

My eyes nearly popped out of my head.

I could confirm that Finn had *not* stuffed anything down his pants that night. The giant rod throbbing in front of me was 100% natural.

This is going to hurt.

I don't care. I looked at him standing there: butt naked. *What a god.* And to think I was going to turn *this* down? *Crazy.* Look at him. His body was perfect. I couldn't wait to feel that giant rod inside me.

I reached over to my glass on the table, knocked back the wine in one, and then snatched the condom out of his hand.

'I'll do it,' I said, tearing the corner of the packet and rolling it on. As I pulled him down on top of me, my elbow caught the bottle of red and sent it crashing to the floor, all over Colette's cream carpet. *Shit.*

'Don't worry,' Finn said, peeling off my knickers and pushing my skirt up around my waist. 'I'll deal with that later. You've told me to fuck you, Roxy, and so that's exactly what I'm going to do. *Right now.*'

Before I'd even had a chance to catch my breath, Finn thrust inside me. I gasped. *God, he's huge.* I'm not going to lie. It was a little painful at first, but I soon got over it and we found our rhythm. I wrapped my legs around his back as we rocked back and forth. I gripped onto his firm arse and pushed him deeper and deeper. *Good Lord! This feels fucking amazing!*

All this time. *All this time.* I'd been withering away in that sham of a marriage and my body had been starved of this. Of these incredible sensations. This is what I'd wanted. Dreamt about. For years. *Decades.* And now it was actually happening, I'd better make the most of it.

I lifted my legs higher and wrapped them around his neck. *Oh yes. Now I can feel him even more.* I ran my hands along his back. His skin was so smooth. So firm. So youthful.

As he moved in and out, his fingers gently circled my clit, building the pressure with every stroke. How did he know to touch me there? *That's the spot. Yes. Oh yes. Oh my God...*

I could feel it happening. I wasn't ready for this to end yet, but I couldn't stop it. As the blood began pumping through my body, I felt dizzy. My brain grew fuzzy and fireworks started sparking inside me.

'Don't you fucking stop, Finn. *Yes! Yes! Yes!* Oh *fuuuu-uuuckk*!!' I screamed.

Finn thrust harder and harder and harder before exploding inside me, then collapsing on my chest.

Wow.

That was...that was...*mind-blowing.*

Shit.

An *actual* orgasm given to me by a man and *not* my vibrator or my own hands.

Jesus.

I felt like a child that had just been introduced to sweets for the first time. In fact, no. *Scrap that.* I thought about that scene in *When Harry Met Sally* where she faked that orgasm. If I imagined that reaction being genuine, with no faking required, then multiplied it by a thousand, *that's* the perfect example of how Finn had just made me feel. And now I wanted us to do it again and again and *again*.

'Thank you,' Finn panted. 'That was even better than I hoped it'd be.'

'Been fantasising about me, have you?' I teased, struggling to catch my breath, whilst trying not to let on how much he had rocked my world. *Can't let him know that was literally the best sex I've ever had. Best to play it cool.* Although, thinking about it, screaming my head off like I just had might have been a dead giveaway…

'Yes! Like every second of the day. Like every time you looked at me at work. My poor dick spent most of the day hitting the top of the desk, you turned me on so much.'

'You mean you were working with a hard-on? *Pervert*!' I cackled.

'Can you blame me?' he said, staring into my eyes. 'You're so sexy. So beautiful.'

Sexy? I blushed. He'd done it again. He kept making my heart do funny fluttery things.

He'd just called me *sexy*.

Might sound lame, but it was hard to explain how it felt to have someone, *anyone*, say that about me. When I was married, most days, I felt like the back end of a bus. Overweight. Frumpy. Ugly. Boring. Like the least attractive person alive.

Steve would never compliment me on my body. In fact, he did everything he could to make me hate it. He'd call me ugly and fat. Tell me I was lucky that he stayed with me and that no other man would want me or treat me as well as he did. And I believed him.

I was at home all day and completely isolated. I didn't go anywhere other than the supermarket on a Friday afternoon or to run errands for him, so the weight did start piling on. But he was hardly slim himself. Yet he acted like he was God's gift. The bigger I got, the more I covered up, wearing tracksuits and baggy tops. I never wanted to show my body. I felt ashamed of it. My confidence hit rock bottom.

I didn't feel like a woman. Like someone any man would actually desire. I didn't even like myself, so how could I expect a guy to? So when I did eventually climb out of that destructive cycle, even when my confidence started to grow again and I took better care of myself and began to feel better, I still had those doubts, those voices niggling away in the back of my head. Wondering if anyone in the universe would ever fancy me again.

Yeah, I'd dreamt about a younger man. *A lot.* But I didn't really think someone like Finn would be interested in me. I mean, whilst I was in pretty good shape now, my boobs weren't as perky as they were in my twenties, and there was no escaping the cellulite on my butt and my thighs, which society loves telling women is unattractive. Yet here I was, sprawled across this posh dining table butt naked, and this hot guy had just said I was sexy. And people could say all they want about how women shouldn't need validation from a man, which was true in theory, but you know what? I didn't care. Everyone, even the most confident women, needed a boost every once in a while and hearing Finn say those words and knowing he meant them had made me feel fucking fantastic.

'Thank you…' I said.

'No thanks necessary. Just stating the facts. And you showing me how banging you looked naked literally two minutes after we met didn't exactly help the constant hard-on situation. I haven't been able to get that vision out of my head ever since.'

'That was *so* embarrassing!' I winced.

'No, it wasn't. You were a vision. You *are* a vision, Roxy. I could look at your body all day,' he said, running his fingers across my breasts, then stroking between my legs.

'It's not *looking* that I want you to do, Finn. I want you to fuck my body all day and all night.' *Crikey.* This Rampant Roxy was certainly a filthy, feisty one. I liked her.

'Do you now?' he teased, nibbling my neck. 'Don't need to ask me twice…whatever happened to sweet honourable Roxy?'

'She's gone away for the weekend,' I said.

'Mmm, and been replaced by *DGAF Roxy*?'

'What's DGAF?'

'Short for *don't give a fuck*.'

'You and your acronyms!' I rolled my eyes.

'Yeah. I know,' he chuckled. 'Just a habit. Well I'm becoming a big fan of this new Roxy…and I'm ready to do exactly what she's asked.'

'You're up for round two again already?'

'*Pretty much.* As you'll discover, one of the many advantages of sleeping with a younger guy is a quicker recovery time and more energy. Well, actually, slight disclaimer, it might not necessarily be the case for *every* guy in their twenties, but it is for me. I can get it up fast and I can go all night. *You'll see...*' He stretched down on the floor to get his wallet, pulled out another condom and put it on the table beside him.

Interesting. I thought men needed much longer to get it up again. Steve could never manage it. It would take him at least an hour or two. And if I was lucky, by that time he would have fallen asleep.

'Promises, promises...' I replied, stroking him, then quickly taking my hand away. I was sure I'd read that some men can't be touched too soon as it's extra sensitive, but Finn didn't flinch. In fact, quite the opposite.

'We have lift-off!' he said, taking my hand and placing it back on him. 'I'm ready for round two when you are...'

Jeez. He wasn't joking. That had sprung up quicker than a water leak.

'Well, then, don't waste time talking, big boy,' I said, reaching for the condom and rolling it on him. 'Hurry up and put that anaconda back inside me.'

'Yes, m'lady!' Finn quipped.

Just as I climbed on top of him, a loud beeping sound went off, and the smell of burning began to flood the room.

'Shit!' Finn jumped up. 'The smoke alarm. I left the pie in the oven!' He leapt to the floor and ran in the kitchen. I quickly followed him.

Finn switched off the oven, then dealt with the alarm.

'That was close!' I said, opening the windows to help the clear the smoke.

'Well, the pie is well and truly cremated,' said Finn, tossing it in the bin, 'but who cares? There are other things we can eat for dessert...' He smirked.

'Oh *really*?' I teased. 'Any suggestions?'

'I can think of a few...in fact, there's another warm

apple pie I'd quite like to taste,' he said, pressing his body against my back and running his hands along my inner thighs. 'And it's not one from a supermarket. I reckon it's a lot sweeter…'

'*Mmm…*' I replied, my mind and body racing. 'That sounds interesting, Finn. Tell me, what exactly did you have in mind?'

'Well,' he said, scooping me into his arms and carrying me up the stairs, 'I could tell you Roxy, but I have a feeling you'll enjoy it *much* more if I show you…'

CHAPTER TEN

I was *exhausted*. But in a good way. Finn wasn't wrong. He definitely was able to go all night.

He'd carried me up to his room and let's just say he showed me his extensive skills. He was very talented with his hands, his tongue, and of course his *anaconda*. I think maybe I'd had about three hours sleep. Four hours, tops. But I wasn't complaining. The more I had him, the more I wanted. I was addicted. I felt like a new woman. A very, very happy and very, very horny woman.

It was like my body was on a mission to make up for lost time all in one night. For all the years that I used to lay underneath Steve like a corpse, wishing it would be over. For all the time I'd spent celibate since starting again. My body had stored everything up, and now it was ready to be unleashed.

I stretched my arms up to the ceiling. Finn had gone downstairs about half an hour ago and it smelt like he was cooking breakfast. *Yum.* I looked around his room. Like the house in general, it had a very neutral colour scheme.

Plain white walls, large wooden bedframe and a thick white duvet with a silver satin trim.

If you'd asked me a week ago what I'd think a twenty-seven-year-old man's bedroom would be like, I would have said it wouldn't be far off a rubbish tip. And with the way Colette doted on him, I would've reckoned Finn would be a bum who left his stuff everywhere for his mum, or rather her cleaner, to pick up after him. But everything was neat and tidy. There were a couple of T-shirts folded on top of the chrome chest of drawers. The white wooden flooring was clean. No junk, empty bottles or glasses. Nothing was out of place. The only things on the floor were condom wrappers.

He was a lot tidier than men my age. And keeping a clean room wasn't the only thing he did better than older guys. Finn was much more skilled in the sack than men almost twice his years. Definitely compared to Terrence and Steve. There was no contest. Finn blew them both out of the water.

When I'd fantasised about getting jiggy with a hot young guy, this was exactly what I'd dreamt of. Rather than holding my nose and cringing as my disgusting, smelly dickhead ex-husband's sweaty pot belly crushed my stomach, I'd always wished I could feel a hunk's tongue roaming all over me. That I could run my hands over his broad shoulders and solid six-pack, stroke his soft youthful skin and thick lustrous hair. I wanted to be blown away by his stamina. His sexual prowess. His keenness to please me.

Ahhh.

Yep. I'd had my first experience with a younger man

and could confirm that it had definitely lived up to my expectations. Just thinking about it made me tingle.

'Breakfast in bed for the sexy lady,' said Finn as he came in clutching a tray. I propped the pillows up behind me. Finn laid it on the bed, took a plate and one of the glasses of what looked like Buck's Fizz off and rested them on the table beside him, then passed the tray to me.

'A full English!' I said, putting the tray on my lap. *Wow*. Someone had made *me* breakfast for a change. 'A man after my own heart.' I smiled. 'Thanks, Finn!'

Careful, Rox. I know no man's ever made you brekkie before, but don't get too gushy. Remember, there can be no 'hearts' involved. This is just sex. Nothing more. Don't start catching feelings.

'And the tomatoes and mushrooms are halved, not diced!' I gushed.

'Diced?' Finn frowned. 'Sorry, I didn't know you liked them to be *diced*. Do you want me to do that for you?'

'No! No! Definitely not! It's just something my ex used to insist on making me do. Don't worry. You don't want to hear about him.'

'No, go on. I'm curious now.' He climbed under the sheets and then stroked my face. 'Tell me. Only if you don't mind, of course.'

'It's okay. Basically, he demanded a full English. Every day. It always had to be piping hot and served at exactly 7.30 a.m. Even on weekends.'

'A full English everyday?' Finn's eyes popped out of his head. 'Once in a while, like today, is fine. Everything in moderation and all that, but *Jesus*. His arteries must be more clogged than a blocked drain. Sorry, go on.'

'Anyway, he was anal about everything. The eggs and bacon had to be cooked in a certain way, the toast had to be a particular shade of brown, not too dark and not too light, and I could never serve the mushrooms or tomatoes whole or halved. They would *have* to be diced into small pieces. It was like I was feeding a bloody one-year-old. Same for whenever I served him lunch or dinner. Apart from peas, every vegetable had to be chopped up. If they weren't done the way he expected, he'd go mental, throw the plate on the floor, then demand I start again and do it "properly" this time.'

'Jesus. He sounds like a complete nutter. A narcissist. Was the abuse physical too?'

'Well, although he never hit me, there was always the feeling that he *could* at any time if I didn't do as I was told and stick to his rules. I was always walking on eggshells.'

'God. I'm so glad you're away from all that. If I'd known it would have brought back those memories, I would have made something different. I can make you some pancakes or avocado on toast or something instead if you like?'

'That's really sweet, but don't worry. It's fine. Forget about him. Let's get back to having fun. After we eat, of course. I really appreciate you bringing me breakfast. Thank you so much.'

'You're welcome,' he said, showering my shoulders with kisses. 'And I'm glad you're up for having some more fun, but yes, it's a good idea to eat first. We've got to keep your strength up. I'm not done with you yet…'

'Glad to hear it,' I said, reaching between his legs.

'Mmm. Although, on second thoughts, we can always postpone the eating part? I'm ready to resume if you are…'

'You're like the bloody Energizer Bunny!' I laughed.

'The what?'

Oh, of course. Those adverts were probably before his time. I must remember that being younger, he was probably not going to get a lot of references I made. *Actually, I think that advert still exists, doesn't it? Oh, who cares?*

'Never mind, it's just an old advertising campaign. Speaking of advertising, or rather marketing, what's your story? You can't have learnt everything from doing a few summers working at the company.'

'I've done internships every summer since I was sixteen at different brands as well as at Mum's business, and these past few years I've had several marketing roles.'

'So is that where you're going to work now? For one of the businesses you've worked at before?'

'I could have, and I was head-hunted by some massive brands who were offering me a lot of money and perks, but I want to use my marketing skills to do something good. The company I'm going to work for is much smaller and not as well paid, but they create tasty healthy food not just for adults, but for kids too. Childhood obesity is so high these days and they're really passionate about creating campaigns to tackle it. We can't stop kids or even adults from eating snacks, so the idea is to provide them with healthier alternatives that taste great. They also donate a portion of sales of every product to give back to children's charities and I'm going to be involved in creating new initiatives too, so I'm really looking forward to it.'

Gosh. Just when I thought I had him sussed, Finn always surprised me. I'd assumed, again wrongly, that because he came from money, he'd either expect his parents to pay his way throughout life or snap up whatever job involved the least amount of work and paid the most money. But he was a really genuine, kind and caring guy.

Without even realising it, I started stroking him.

'Mmm…that feels great. Ready to go again?'

'Tempting,' I said as I continued, 'but maybe we should stick to the original plan. I'll be ready as soon as I've eaten. Can't let this good food you've made go to waste.'

'If you insist,' he said, reaching for his plate. 'But, if you keep touching me, I'm going to find it hard to resist jumping on top of you. *Just saying…*'

'Okay,' I said, removing my hand. 'Time out. So,' I said, placing the fried egg on top of the toast and taking a bite, 'I'm curious. Am I the first older woman you've been with?' I thought about the conversation I'd had with Colette and that older woman at the office.

'Not exactly,' he said, swallowing a mouthful of food. 'There's been a few…'

'Hmm…so you like a seasoned lady?' I cackled.

'You could say that. I've dated women my age too, though.'

'And do you find a difference?'

'Generally speaking, yeah. I prefer someone older. Women in their thirties or forties are more confident. They've got their shit together. They're more emotionally stable. Wiser. They don't want to play games. They know who they are, what they want both in and out of the bedroom, and they're not afraid to tell you. They just go for it. There's less BS. And I'm all for that.'

'Interesting,' I said. I'd never looked at it like that before. I'd just thought that every man dreamt of screwing a younger woman. I'd been so used to women over forty being seen by society as over the hill and ready for the scrap heap, which was utter bollocks. So it was nice to hear that some men appreciated us.

'And you?' asked Finn. 'I take it from your initial resistance, I'm your first YM?'

'Another one of your acronyms!' I rolled my eyes.

'Sorry. Younger Man.'

'Yep, that's right.' *In real life, anyway.* I'd fantasised about loads of younger men, but never had the chance to make it happen in reality. *Until now.*

'And…?'

'*And*…you and your giant pole have flown the flag for the *YM* society very well, Finn,' I said, running my hands all over his chest, along the happy trail of hair leading from his belly button all the way down past his waist, then wrapping my hand around him again. I couldn't help myself. 'You're an excellent ambassador. But I'm sure that by the way you've been making me come, that was obvious…'

'Well, a man's only as good as the last orgasm he gave, so I can't rest on my laurels. Got to keep you satisfied.'

'Cheers to that!' I raised the glass of Buck's Fizz, clinking it against his. 'So,' I said, putting the tray on the bedside table, 'I've had a good feed now, I'm feeling much better, and it looks like your flag is flying at full mast, so what do you say we get back to it and you help to satisfy my appetite in other ways?'

'I say *I like your thinking…*' Finn said as he tossed the duvet covers off. Just as he climbed on top of me, there was a loud bang.

For God's sake. Last night it was the smoke alarm, and now there was another interruption. 'What was that?'

I said, trying to listen out. 'Was that the front door?' I froze. I heard more noises. There was definitely someone downstairs. 'Shit, shit, shit!' I jumped up as the realisation hit me. 'Is your mum back already? Shit!' My heart raced.

Clothes. I need clothes! I scanned the room. My knickers and skirt were on the dining room table, and if I remembered correctly, my bra was last seen on the kitchen floor. God knows where I'd left my top.

'Shit!' I repeated, this time whispering. 'I can't let Colette find us in bed together. *No way!*'

Looks like honourable Roxy was back in the building. *Dammit.*

'Chill, Rox,' said Finn, putting his hands behind his head. 'If it's Mum, then don't worry about it. I'll talk to her. Who cares what she thinks? It's not like I'm underage and you're some woman who has taken advantage of me. She's got to accept that I can sleep with whoever I want.'

'You just don't get it, do you?' I snapped, still frantically trying to think of what I could put on.

The only clothes in here naturally were Finn's. It wouldn't exactly look good if I came downstairs wearing his T-shirt, would it?

I scanned the room again. I spotted a towel. That could work. I snatched it off the radiator, wrapped it round me, cracked his bedroom door to check that the coast was clear and then crept outside.

I glanced down the stairwell. It was Colette sitting on the bottom step. What was she doing back so soon? It was barely 1 p.m.

Think quickly. Think!

I might be able to make it back to my room without her

seeing me. I took another few steps and was almost at my door when the floorboard creaked. Colette glanced up.

'Roxy?' she called out. *Shit.*

'Oh, hi, Colette!' I said, heading towards the top of the stairs. *Jeez.* I didn't realise my voice could go that high. *Calm down and act natural.* 'I wasn't expecting you back so early. Is everything okay?'

'Did you just wake up?' She frowned, looking me up and down in the towel.

'No, I—I, er…' *Think, for God's sake, think!* 'I went for a run and I was just about to get into the shower when I heard the door, so I thought I'd come and investigate. You know, you can never be too careful. Intruders and all that!'

'That's true. You should have just called Finn.' Colette seemed off. Not her normal chirpy self. 'Speaking of which, where is Finn?'

'Finn?' I said nervously.

'Yes, have you seen him?'

'No, no, I haven't…' *God I hate lying.* 'I'm not sure if he's up yet. No idea.' *Okay, enough now. She's got the message. Less is more.*

'Oh. I thought I heard his voice when I came in.' *Shit. How is that even possible? Has she got supersonic ears?* I hoped she hadn't heard our conversation. Well, clearly she couldn't have done as I was still alive. 'Typical. He's probably still in bed. *Honestly.* He hasn't changed since he was a teenager. He could always sleep late into the afternoon. Even if there was an earthquake, nothing would wake him. He may be twenty-seven, but he'll still always be the same old Finn. My baby boy.'

Oh God. Could you imagine if she knew that Finn hadn't been sleeping at all because he'd been too busy fucking my brains out? I lowered my head. I couldn't face looking her in the eyes.

'Anyway, Roxy, to answer your question, no, I'm far from okay. I had a massive argument with Donald, so I took a flight back this morning. I couldn't bear to stay with him a minute longer.'

'Sorry to hear that. Do you want to talk about it?'

'Not really, I'm too angry. I'm just going to take my shoes off and make a cup of tea and work out what to do after that.' She got up and started to walk towards the kitchen.

'No!' I shouted, freaking out at the prospect of her finding my bra on the floor. Pretty sure I'd taken Finn's T-shirt off in there too, so if she saw both of them in a heap on the tiles, it wouldn't take her long to work out what we'd been up to. 'No way! Sounds like you've had a stressful time. Why don't you go upstairs and have a nice shower? That'll make you feel better, and then I'll bring a cuppa and some biscuits up to your room.'

'Would you?' Colette's eyes lit up.

'Of course!'

'That would be wonderful! Nice to know there's someone I can trust and rely on. Not like Donald. *Men!* I'll go up and shower right now. You're an angel.'

An angel? *Far from it.*

Normally I'd be blown away to have Colette say something which resembled gratitude, but I was certain that if I knocked on heaven's door right now, God would send me packing with a one-way ticket straight to hell.

All of the strength and DGAF gusto I had been filled with last night had quickly evaporated. Now that I'd done the deed, in the cold light of day, I wasn't feeling so confident about standing up to her and telling her that she could stick her opinions because Finn and I could do what we wanted. Without the high of the alcohol mixed with all that horniness and sexual desire, I could see now that it just wasn't that simple.

If only she knew. If Colette knew what we'd been doing, at best she'd kick me out and of course fire me. At worst, she'd fucking kill me. Probably chop me up into tiny pieces and feed me to a pack of starving wolves.

That's why last night was definitely a one-off. Finn and I couldn't hook up again. As of right now, things needed to go back to the way they had been twenty-four hours ago. We had to keep our relationship strictly professional. And most important of all, Colette could never find out that we'd slept together.

Ever.

CHAPTER ELEVEN

'Well, personally, I think you should continue sleeping with Finn and tell Colette to like it or lump it. You're a grown woman and he's a grown man, for God's sake. She needs to learn she can't keep mollycoddling him,' said Alex as she poured me another glass of rosé.

I'd been at her flat for the past couple of hours and was filling her in on what had happened with Finn and Colette earlier this afternoon.

After I'd suggested I make Colette a cup of tea, I'd only just managed to pick up our clothes and stash them in my laundry basket upstairs, then make the kitchen and dining room look semi-decent again before she'd come back downstairs. Normally, whenever I got in the shower, it was hard for me to drag myself out again, so I wasn't expecting her to have finished that quickly.

Finn had come down not long after Colette, holding the tray. I'd panicked, hoping to God that he wasn't bringing down two plates and two champagne flutes, which would definitely have been a red flag. Thankfully, there was only his plate of half-eaten food on there. No glasses. Not sure where he'd put them. I was just grateful that we were on the same page and covering our tracks.

I thought we were in the clear until Colette decided she'd take her tea and sit in the dining room with the Sunday papers.

"What the hell happened in here!" she'd shouted. Finn and I had both glared at each other.

I'd picked up the clothes, the condoms wrappers, wiped down the table…what had I missed? We'd both walked into the room, ready to accept our fate.

"My carpet! Look at it!" she'd screamed.

I'd totally forgotten. We were supposed to sort that, but obviously we'd got sidetracked. In the end, Finn told Colette that after I'd gone upstairs to have an early night, he'd stayed in the dining room, got carried away with drinking and knocked the bottle off the table. He said he'd planned to clean it up once he'd slept off his hangover, but he wasn't expecting Colette back so soon.

She'd moaned about the fact that it would be a nightmare to get red wine out of a cream carpet, but in the end Colette believed him. I felt relieved. I'd gone back to the kitchen to try and find something to attempt to get the stain out, and Finn came in and tried to kiss me. But after going with the flow for a few seconds—okay, maybe more than a few—I'd pushed him away and told him it was too risky. His mum was in the next room, for God's sake. I said we had to stop. I knew I needed to get out of there. Away from him. Away from temptation. So I'd got dressed and come straight here to see Alex.

'I agree,' I sighed. 'Well, I mean the bit about Finn

being a grown man and Colette being overprotective. I really wish I could tell her to sod off, but I can't rock the boat.'

'Aaarggh!' Alex slapped her forehead. 'Not this rocking the boat rubbish again, Roxy! Look: I know Colette bailed you out and helped you get away from your prick of an ex-husband, but that doesn't mean you should keep letting her walk all over you.'

'She doesn't…' I sighed, knowing that it was probably true, but not wanting to admit it. 'I know she's demanding and a pain sometimes, but—'

'Oh, come on! She sends you to run her errands for her when she's got a perfectly competent PA, and she dumps last-minute meetings and demands on you. She's your boss, so she's in charge of you at work, then, because she's your landlady, she's also in charge of your home. But are you really going to start letting her control your sex life too? Don't you see? It might sound a bit extreme, but in some ways she's like Steve.'

'Come on, Alex!' I scoffed. 'That's taking it *way* too far. Colette is nothing like that dickhead! He was a completely controlling arsehole. I wasn't allowed to leave the house, speak to friends or family. He convinced me that everyone was bad and he was the only person I needed. Changed my phone number so you couldn't contact me. Called the house phone at different times every afternoon to check I was in the house. Brainwashed me into doing everything he told me to.'

'Yes, he was at the extreme end of the scale. And I know she doesn't tell you to make sure her cup of tea is beside the bed at a set time, or demand that the shower is turned on at precisely 6.40 a.m. or whatever it was to make sure it was perfectly warm like he did, but you still do everything that Colette asks you to! And now you've got a hot guy who is besotted with you and is giving you the best sex of your life, and instead of rolling around in bed with him, you're here hiding out at my flat like a teenager because you're too scared to fess up to sleeping with another consenting adult. It's not right.'

She had a point. I did feel like I was fifteen years old, sneaking a boy into the house, worried that my parents might find out and ground me. And at the grand age of forty-one, that wasn't how I wanted to live my life. But what else could I do? This was the situation I found myself in, and as frustrating as it was, I had to play by the rules until I was in a better position.

'I have to think of the bigger picture. Staying with Colette is helping me to save up to buy my own house, so I can't afford to piss her off. And, yes, Finn is amazing in bed, but he's only here for another week, so I need to think with my head and not my libido and remind myself that it's not worth throwing my career and everything down the toilet for a fling. Surely you can see that?'

'I can, but I just don't like the way she has you jumping through hoops all the time. It's like she knows that because she helped you, she can literally ask you to do anything and you'll never refuse, and that's still a form of control. I think you should start learning to say no. Stand up to her a bit more. That's all I'm saying.'

Sounded good and easy in theory, but the reality was a whole different story. Colette wouldn't understand. I mean, most bosses wouldn't want their employees to hook up together at all, never mind with one that also happened to be their beloved child. So given that Colette had already told me her views on Finn and women, particularly *older* women, expecting her to roll out the red carpet and be cool with it all just wasn't going to happen.

'I'll think about it, Alex. I'll try and start setting some boundaries at work and at home. But as hard as it's going to be, I also need to put an end to this fling, because I know if I don't, it's going to all end in tears.'

CHAPTER TWELVE

'You skipped breakfast,' said Finn, placing a paper Pret a Manger bag on my desk whilst expertly juggling two coffees on top of a stack of glass containers filled with food.

Damn, he looked good in his crisp pale blue shirt and smart dark trousers. It was the first time I'd seen him since Sunday. I had been doing everything I could to avoid him these past few days and, until now, had managed to pull it off.

On Monday, I'd had to focus on the sales side of my job and not the show, so I was out at meetings all day, then went straight to Alex's in the evening and stayed over again like I had on Sunday night.

On Tuesday, Finn had asked if he could work remotely as he wanted to go to Liverpool and spend the day with his gran at the hospital because he was worried about the fact that she was still poorly. Later that day, he'd also messaged to ask if I was deliberately avoiding him and I'd replied to say I thought it was best that we kept our distance. He told me that he didn't agree and he wanted to talk. But he didn't get home until really late, so we'd missed seeing each other again.

And now here we were today. Wednesday. The first time that I'd had to see him face-to-face. I'd woken up extra early this morning so that we wouldn't bump into each other at home, but he was already awake and cooking something in the kitchen, so I'd slipped out the front door. But now we were in the office. Together. All alone. Just inches apart, and he was looking so tempting.

Fuck.

'Here,' he said, reaching into the bag with his spare hand. How he was managing to balance all the other stuff at the same time, I didn't know. 'I got you a chocolate croissant. Thought I'd better avoid anything related to a full English this time. I also got you a coffee with extra milk, just the way you like it.' He put the cups down, lifted one out of the cardboard carrier, placed it next to the bag, then lined up the glass containers beside it. 'And because I know you won't have time to go to lunch today, I made some for you. Not a chicken salad sandwich, though, like you normally have, as the bread will make you tired in the afternoon, but chicken with fresh vegetables and brown rice, which will help keep your energy levels up. Then this little dish has some apples, sliced, not diced, for you to snack on or if you need something sweet.'

I didn't know what to say.

He'd done all of this for me? Getting up early to cook for me? Especially after he must have got home so late last night?

My stomach began to flutter. He was so kind.

Stop it! Don't start getting all mushy. Just say thank you.

'Finn, that's…that's so…really, really thoughtful. Thanks so much. You didn't have to…'

'No big deal.' He shrugged his shoulders. 'I do really need to talk to you, though, Roxy. Can we…'

Just as he was about to finish his sentence, my office phone rang. *Saved by the bell.*

'Sorry, I have to get this. I'm expecting a call from the stand designers.'

He picked up his coffee cup and one of the glass containers and went over to his desk. I could see from the corner of my eye that he was grinding his teeth. He was annoyed that I wouldn't talk to him, but it was for the best.

By the time I'd finished the call, the office had started to fill up. *Thank God.* As long as I was here, surrounded by other people, keeping my head down and focusing on my work, it would be fine. Everything would be under control.

Pff. If only. Something told me that keeping Finn from my thoughts was not going to be so simple…

'Can I come and show you something, Roxy?' said Finn.

What? Nooo. No, no, no.

It was now after six and I'd managed to stay calm around him. Well, sort of. We'd kept a professional distance and avoided speaking for most of the day. So far I'd been strong, but there was no way I could have him coming over here to my desk, standing next to me, looking all sexy. I couldn't cope.

'Can you just email me, please? I'm busy. I've decided I'm going to Manchester tonight, and I still have some things to finish first.'

The truth was, I didn't really need to go up tonight. I could easily go tomorrow evening, but I needed to stay away from him and I thought travelling to another city was the only way to do that right now.

'It won't take a second,' he said, ignoring me, then pulling up a chair beside mine.

God, he's so close. And now he was staring. He only had to look at me and he sent me into a spin.

'So what do you think of this?' he said, leaning forward and pointing to a car advert in a magazine.

What the hell? How was this relevant or important?

'Why are you…'

'Shhh…' he said as he ran his hands up my legs and in between my thighs.

'What are you doing?' I shouted a bit too loudly, pushing his hand away and swinging my head around nervously to see if anyone was left in the office and had seen. I could see Julie in the distance, and Warren was just heading out of the door. *Colette!* Her light was on in her office. *Jesus.* What was he thinking?

'Stop it! I whispered. 'Like I said in my messages, we can't do this! Anyone could have seen us. Your mum is still here, for God's sake.'

'I don't care. I want you, Roxy,' he said, drawing me in with those hypnotic eyes. 'You've been avoiding me for days, and not being able to touch you is driving me crazy.'

'Look,' I said, pushing the wheelie chair back to create some distance, 'Saturday night was great, but it's over, Finn. We can't. It's just not possible.'

'But, Roxy—'

'Like I've said so many times before, you need to understand that it's not feasible.'

'What's not feasible?'

I looked up to see Colette standing by my desk, doing something on her mobile.

Shit. Had she flown here from her office? I hoped that was the only thing she'd heard.

'Noth—nothing…' I said.

'So, how's everything shaping up for the show?' she asked. *Phew.* She must have been on her phone as she'd walked towards us and only caught the last few words of our conversation.

'Yep, everything's under control. I'm getting the train up to Manchester tonight so I can check out the venue again tomorrow and be around for when the stand people arrive, but all the stock and brochures we sent up from the office arrived safely, and Maggie and Jeremy will be checking into the hotel on Friday afternoon and have already been briefed, so it's all good.'

'Wonderful!' Colette beamed. 'I told you that you could do it. I said you and Finn would make a good team.'

'We do, don't we?' said Finn, staring into my eyes. I looked away quickly before I fell under his spell again.

'Indeed!' said Colette, thankfully not realising that Finn meant something completely different to what she did. 'It's a shame you can't stay longer, darling. Anyway,' she said, composing herself, 'Finn and I will get the train up on Friday evening,'

'Or I could go earlier?' Finn suggested. 'Y'know, to help Roxy set up.'

'It's fine,' I jumped in. 'Like I said, it's all under

control. I'll give you a call tomorrow, Colette, and send you some photos on Friday once the stand is set up so you can see how it all looks before you arrive.'

'Good. When you get there tomorrow, could you be a darling and check the spa's availability for an express facial and mani-pedi for either their last appointment in the evening or before the show starts first thing on Saturday morning, so I can look fresh?'

For God's sake.

'Sure,' I said, gritting my teeth. *Honestly.* Talk about lastminute.com. Sometimes I wondered what Raquel did, as it felt like Colette asked me to do *everything*. It was like I was her skivvy. And she never said please or thank you. It was always *would you be a darling this* or *would you be a darling that.* So annoying. One of these days I'd love to say: 'Would *you* be a darling and do it your bloody self!'

No, no. Mustn't be ungrateful.

'Wonderful!' Colette gushed. 'See you on Friday.'

I watched Colette drive off from the car park and breathed a sigh of relief. Aside from her adding more stuff to my to-do list, it was at least good that another close call had been avoided. My nerves couldn't take much more of this. If I wanted to get my adrenaline going, I'd go on a roller coaster. It'd be a lot less stressful.

'Roxy,' Finn said softly.

'Press releases!' I shouted, jumping up from my seat. 'I forgot to print the press releases for our most recent launches!'

'It's okay. All the press releases are on the memory sticks we sent to Alex's people to put in the press office. These days, everything's paperless. Can we—'

'I know, I know, but I still wanted some hard copies. To give to more traditional customers or journalists who aren't into all the digital stuff. Can you grab some paper for the colour printer from the stationery cupboard for me, please?'

'Can we talk first? Please?'

'Finn.' I scowled. 'We're at work and this is important. I need to print these releases out now before I forget again.'

'Sure,' he huffed, getting up from the chair and heading over to the cupboard.

Once he was out of sight, I felt my shoulders relax a little and exhaled. I thought I'd done a good job of holding it together today. By that, I mean I'd resisted jumping across the desk and straight onto his lap. I had things under control. Until he'd touched me. And now him fucking me was all I could think about.

Whenever Finn was around me, I couldn't breathe. I could already feel the tingling down under. I wanted him so badly. As soon as those releases were printed, either he had to go straight home or I had to go back to the house, throw some stuff in my suitcase, then head straight to the station, as we couldn't stay in the same space together. Not when there were so few people left in the office. Not when our desks and our bodies would be inches apart. He was just too hot to resist.

I finished typing out an email and clicked send. *That's it.* I was pretty much done for the day. I was feeling good. *Calm.* It had been touch and go for weeks, but now, I was confident that the show would go well. Finn had been a massive help. Speaking of Finn, where was he with that glossy paper? Those releases were the last thing to tick off my list before I headed off, and he was holding me up. I grabbed my phone and texted him.

Me

Sometime this century, please! What's taking so bloody long?

Actually, what if he doesn't have his phone with him?

Finn

CFI

Of course he has his phone with him. *Bloody millennials.*

Me

CFI?

Finn

Can't find it.

Me

I saw it there on Friday. Can't be finished already.

Finn

IDK what to tell you

Finn

IDK=I don't know

For fuck's sake. *If you want something done, you've got to do it yourself,* I thought as I stormed off towards the cupboard. I stepped inside and saw it straight away. On the first shelf, next to the normal copier paper. *What the hell? Is he blind? In fact, where is he?*

As I turned around, Finn stepped inside and shut the door behind him.

'Finn…what are you doing?'

'Well, if you're going to keep ignoring me, then I had to find a way to get you alone.'

I stomped towards the door. 'Move out of the way, Finn.'

'Nope, sorry. No can do.'

'You can't hold me in here against my will,' I said, standing in front of him and trying to push him aside.

'It's not against your will if you want me, and I know you do, Roxy. Don't fight it.'

He picked me up, pushed me against the wall and planted his lips firmly on mine. My knees buckled.

'We can't…' I whispered feebly.

'Shh…we *can*…relax…' My lips parted willingly and he slid his tongue inside. I reciprocated as he flicked it against mine. Finn started kissing my neck, unbuttoned my blouse, then pulled the front of my bra down, exposing my breasts. He pushed them together, wrapped his mouth around my nipples and began sucking slowly.

Oh my God.

His hands slipped under my skirt and into my knickers.

I groaned much louder than I should have, but I couldn't help myself. As his tongue began to travel down to my belly button, and he plunged his fingers inside me, I realised that it was pointless trying to resist. My mind could say no a million times, but the truth was that once Finn's mouth was on me, once our bodies were touching, all logic and fears about the consequences of our actions went straight out the window.

Yep. The best thing I could do right now was to forget about everything. Let Rampant Roxy take over and enjoy the ride whilst I could, because if this all blew up in my face and I was left homeless and jobless, I needed to know that at least I'd made the most of these moments whilst they'd lasted.

CHAPTER THIRTEEN

The first day of the show had gone well. *Professionally speaking.* The stand looked great, we'd had so many visitors come to enter the prize draw, and we'd sold out of our electric facial cleansing brushes. I was relieved, and Colette was delighted. The only one who wasn't happy was Finn.

He'd been moody all day. When Colette and Finn had arrived in Manchester late last night, Finn had texted me to ask if he could come to my room. I'd told him we both needed to get some sleep, and then I'd switched off my phone. When I'd woken up, he'd messaged again but I hadn't replied because I was busy getting ready.

He'd caught me alone earlier when I'd finished speaking to a customer and moaned that I was ignoring him. *It's true.* I had been. I didn't want to, but I had no choice. I couldn't have any fuck-ups. I needed laser focus, and whenever he was around, my mind and body turned to bloody jelly. There was no way I could let that happen today. Especially not in front of Colette and the team.

'Roxy,' said Colette, calling me over to the back of the stand. 'Can I have a word, please?' *That sounds ominous.*

'Everything alright?' I asked as confidently as I could.

'It's about Finn,' she said sternly.

Please don't tell me she knows.

'Finn?' I said, trying to stop my eyes from widening. 'What about him?'

'I just wondered if you knew what was wrong with him.' She folded her arms. I wasn't used to Colette being so serious.

'Me?' I said, my heart beating faster. 'Why me? I mean why, what would you, how would…' *Stop stuttering, for God's sake.* 'Why do you think I would know?'

'Well, because you've been working closely with him. He's been acting strange ever since I got back from Nice on Sunday. I can't put my finger on why.'

Well, at least I'm in the clear. Thank fuck for that.

'Perhaps he's worried about his gran?'

'No, no. Mum was released from hospital yesterday and is doing fine now, so it's definitely not that.'

'Maybe he's just tired. I mean, we've had a lot to do, lots of late nights,' I said, my mind flashing back to that steamy Saturday evening we'd spent on the dining table and rolling around his bedroom. *I've got to stop thinking about it.*

'No, no, it's not that. He's snappy. He has these mood swings. One minute he's up, the next he's down. Something's off. Call it mother's intuition. I remember him being like this when that Ruth was on the scene.' *Gosh.* She really didn't like that woman, did she? 'When they were getting on, it was like he'd won the lottery, but if they'd had an argument, he was like a bear with a sore head. *Oh God.* I hope she's not back on the scene again. I hope they haven't got back in touch. If she, or any other girl hurts my son again, it'll be the last thing they do…' she scowled. Protective Colette was pretty scary.

Message heard loud and clear. Exactly why I was keeping my distance from now on.

I wondered what had happened with this Ruth woman and Finn to make Colette hate her so much. Then again, knowing how overprotective Colette was, it could have been something stupid, like just seeing them kiss. *Honestly. She needs to get a grip.* Anyway, it didn't matter. It was none of my business. Finn and I were just a one-night thing (well, two if you counted the stationery cupboard) and now because I was trying to do the right thing and put an end to it so we could avoid everything from blowing up in our faces, he was sulking.

'Do you think she came round that Saturday night? You stayed in, didn't you? Did you hear anyone come in? To his room?'

Jesus. Now I have to lie again. I really don't want to, but sometimes you have to do bad things to survive.

'I, er…no, I don't think so, but I went to bed early and was out like a log, so I honestly don't know.' Did I honestly just use the word *honestly*? I know I was trying to be convincing, but that was *definitely* a step too far.

'Hmm,' said Colette, resting her finger on her chin. 'Maybe I can get him to talk when we go out for dinner tonight, just the three of us.'

'Sorry, what? Dinner?' my blood ran cold.

'Yes: you, me and Finn.'

Hell no.

'Thanks, Colette, but I'm just heading off to the

exhibitors' welcome drinks now, so I won't be able to make it.'

'That's fine.' She rested her hand gently on my shoulder. 'So are we. We'll go to dinner afterwards.'

'I've already arranged to meet up with a few business contacts,' I lied again. This was becoming a habit. 'Is it okay if I let you know later?'

'That's fine.'

Phew.

'Thanks,' I said, walking quickly towards the exit. *That's that, then.* Now I knew I'd need to stay at that drinks party for long as possible. Anything to avoid going to dinner with them, because that was guaranteed to be a disaster. One that I had to avoid at all costs…

'Trudy! Great to see you,' I said, striding across the dark wooden floors of the fancy cocktail bar to get out of speaking to Finn. I'd been dodging him since he'd arrived. I was hoping that I could stick with Alex all night, but understandably, she had to schmooze with all of her clients. Thankfully, Finn headed off to get a drink instead.

It was only a matter of time before he cornered me, though, so I needed to line up someone else to speak to. Trudy was one of the event organisers who worked with Alex, so I was sure she could introduce me to some people.

Of course! *Brainwave.*

'Trudy, I'm looking for a PR agency. Anyone here tonight that you could recommend?'

'There *is*, actually. Sophia Huntingdon. She runs an

agency called BEcome, and the whole team there are brilliant. If you give me your card, I can pass it on to her if you like.'

I saw Finn pick up his drink and start walking towards me.

'Um, better still, can we see if we can find her right now? I'd really like to chat to someone tonight so we can take on an agency as quickly as possible.'

'Sure!' she said. 'Actually, I've just spotted her.'

'Great! Let's go,' I said as we walked past Finn. He scowled at me.

I don't know why he keeps sulking. Couldn't he understand that I wasn't ignoring him because I didn't like him? It was the exact opposite. Did I think about him more than I should? *Yes.* Did I wish that we could sneak off into the toilets right now and have a repeat performance of that session where he'd fucked me in the stationery cupboard? *Most definitely.* Was I going to act on those feelings? *Hell no.* I would do the right thing, go and speak to this PR woman, and then I'd suggest to Colette that they leave and have dinner without me.

'Roxy, this is Sophia. Sophia, this is Roxy, Sales and Marketing Manager for Cole Beauty Solutions, a health and beauty tools company. Roxy's looking for a PR agency, and so naturally I said she needed to speak to you!'

'Great!' Sophia smiled warmly. 'Lovely to meet you, Roxy, and thanks for the recommendation.'

'No worries!' said Trudy. 'I'll leave you both to it.'

With her glossy, smooth dark hair, flawless make-up and perfectly fitted emerald dress and red-bottom heels, she certainly looked the part. There wasn't anything out of place. *Jeez. Must take her ages to get ready in the morning.*

I gave Sophia a brief overview on our objectives for the launch of our new Sonic Pulse Technology electric toothbrushes, and she suggested a ballpark figure of how much it was likely to cost and said she'd send over a proposal with ideas of how her team could help the products get mass exposure. Sophia seemed smart and definitely knew her stuff. I had a good feeling about her.

After we finished talking about the project, we got some more drinks and found a quieter corner with a glossy black table and a couple of sleek black leather stools. I don't know how, but we got onto the subject of divorce and relationships. *Oh yes. That's it.* Because we were talking about high-end toothbrushes and the difference in the results they delivered compared to the manual ones, I mentioned how my disgusting shithead ex-husband only changed his plastic toothbrush every year. Then, before I could stop myself, I was telling her all about what a controlling arsehole he was and how glad I was to be away from him.

'Sounds like it was a very difficult marriage. I really admire you for having the strength to walk away from your relationship, though. Can't have been easy. If you don't mind me asking, what gave you the courage to finally leave?'

'Thanks. You're right, it wasn't easy. I existed in that toxic bubble for a decade, and then one day, I was watching a morning TV show and the hosts were interviewing a woman who was raising awareness of narcissistic abuse and speaking about a relationship she was in for over twenty years. She explained that because the signs are invisible and often don't include physical things like bruises, that type of abuse is harder to spot.'

'That's so true. Did she mention something that made you think her experiences were similar to yours?'

'Yeah, that's exactly what happened. When she started talking about the things her husband used to do and say, the way he used to control her, isolated her from her family and chipped away at her self-esteem, alarm bells started ringing. It was like I'd been living in a dark room and suddenly someone switched on a light.'

'So what did you do then? Pack a suitcase and leave straight away, or was it a slower, more gradual process?'

'God! I wish I'd had the balls to up and leave there and then!' I took a sip of Prosecco. 'But it wasn't that easy. Even then, when I finally realised that there was a problem, I didn't do anything about it. I couldn't. I didn't know how. I couldn't see how I could ever leave him. I had no money, hadn't spoken to my friends for years. I kept asking myself, where would I go? What would I do?'

'What about your parents?' She frowned. 'Wouldn't they have helped you?'

As if, I said to myself. Mum had disowned me after I'd gotten married. Partly because I hadn't told her, but mainly because it wasn't in a church. "Imagine what people would say," she'd said. As for my dad, he was a weak man who did anything Mum told him to. Hadn't spoken to them in years. *No big loss*. My mum was horrible and strict growing up. I couldn't wait to escape. That was one of the things that Alex and I had in common. Neither of us got on with our parents. Or most of our family, to be honest. Although she couldn't understand it, I actually liked Alex's mum. She was always very liberal and free-spirited. The complete opposite of mine.

'Pff! Apart from Alex, I don't really have any contact with my family. They're all giant pains in the arse, so that wasn't an option.'

I wasn't sure what had come over me to make my tongue so loose (the tequila we'd drunk earlier and the fact that I'd also been drinking Prosecco, gin and God knows what else all evening might have had something to do with it), but I just couldn't stop spilling my guts. I don't normally open up to people I've just met, but somehow we just clicked. Sophia was really easy to talk to. I know talking about your personal life isn't the most professional way to act during a first meeting, but something told me I could trust her and that she was the kind of person I could see becoming my friend.

'Oh, I see…sorry to hear that.'

'Don't be. Anyway, I only realised how bad things had got when Steve's company relocated. We moved back to North London, and I bumped into Colette, told her what I was going through and she said she'd help. That's when I started making plans to divorce Steve and began the long journey of getting my life back on track.'

'Wow, Roxy.' Sophia's eyes widened. 'You're incredible. A real inspiration.'

'Well, I don't know about that, but nice of you to say so. Thanks.'

Just as I was about to ask Sophia whether she was single like me or all loved up, Finn came over. Talk about rubbish timing.

'Hi,' he said, smiling at Sophia. 'I'm Finn, I work with Roxy. Would you excuse us for a moment, please?'

'Actually, Finn,' I chimed in before she had a chance to reply, 'Sophia and I are having a really important conversation, so can we catch up tomorrow on the stand, please?' I plastered on a fake grin, then gave him a *what are you playing at?* glare. 'Oh, look, there's Colette. Colette!' I called out, and she began walking towards us. Finn started grinding his teeth. Yes, yes, I could see he was pissed off, but he was looking ridiculously hot tonight in a slim-cut sharp blue suit, with his crisp fitted open-neck white shirt teasing me by showing off a bit of his solid chest. If he cornered me, we'd end up screwing in the toilets, and I didn't fancy becoming the talk of the industry when someone inevitably caught us.

'We're off to dinner now, Roxy, will you join us?' asked Colette.

'Actually, I've just met an amazing PR woman, Sophia. Sophia, this is Colette, our MD.' They both shook hands. 'And so I'm going to stay here so that we can chat about the project and how she can help us make it a success.'

'Nice to meet you, Sophia.' Colette gave an approving nod. 'That sounds exciting! Okay, Roxy, no problem. In that case, we'll see you bright and early on the stand tomorrow. But if you change your mind, just call me and I'll let you know where to find us.'

'Will do,' I said, knowing I absolutely would not. Finn scowled at me again as he left. *Good God.* Even when he was giving me a dirty look, he was still so sexy. *Fuck.*

'Well, he's cute!' Sophia grinned as she watched him leave. I found myself feeling a slight pang of jealousy. Or maybe it was just indigestion. Getting jealous was stupid. More than that: it was utterly *ridiculous.* It wasn't like

Finn was my boyfriend or anything. I shrugged my shoulders, as if I hadn't noticed how incredible he looked tonight, which of course I had. Along with literally every female in the bar. I'd seen their tongues hanging out when he'd walked in. 'Oh, if only I was young, free and single again…' Sophia sighed.

'I take it you're married, then?' I glanced down at her left hand.

'No, not married. In a long-term relationship.'

'And are you happy?'

'Um, well…yes! *Of course* I am!' *If you say so, Sophia.* People who were happy didn't usually wish that they were free and single, I thought. 'I mean, my boyfriend is *nice*,' she continued. 'He's really sweet…and kind and…and…helpful and *handsome*. Yes. He's really nice.'

Sophia doth protest too much.

'But is he fuckable, though?' I replied. Sophia spat out her gin and tonic, then quickly grabbed a tissue from her bag to wipe her mouth. 'Being nice and reliable is all well and good, but do you still have that spark? Does he also give you a good seeing-to in the bedroom?' Her eyes looked like they were about to pop out of her head. 'Sorry, Sophia. *Too far*? Sometimes I have a problem filtering my thoughts before I speak. Especially once I've had a drink,' I cackled. 'You'll get used to it. Although I'm not exactly painting myself in the best light right now, normally I'm *very* professional. *Honest.* Tonight I just feel like letting my hair down. Didn't mean to offend…'

'I'm not offended. You just caught me by surprise!' She burst out laughing. 'I actually really like your straight-talking, Roxy. The way you just say what you think. It's refreshing. And I love how brave you are. Leaving your ex, even though it meant starting from scratch. It takes a lot of courage to walk away from a relationship when you've been together a while.' She took a large gulp of her drink and glanced down at the floor.

Everything about her was polished. *Immaculate.* Her hair. Her make-up. Her clothes. *Everything.* You could tell she had a glamorous life and was super-successful. Yet I also reckoned she was a bit lost too. Her eyes seemed sad. Maybe we had more in common than she thought.

'It does take courage and strength, but it's worth it, Sophia. If you're not happy, don't waste your life.'

'I wasn't talking about *me*,' she protested again. 'I *am* happy. I've got a *great* life. I'm *very* lucky.'

Hmm. I sensed that was what she told herself, but in reality she probably wasn't. Whilst her boyfriend sounded a million times better than Steve, at the same time, it didn't exactly seem like he was the love of her life either. She'd probably settled for the safe option.

Ugh. The thought of being trapped in another unhappy relationship made me want to throw up. Now I'd had a taste of what's out there, I couldn't wait to get stuck in properly. I definitely wasn't looking for anything boring and predictable. Excitement and fun would definitely be on my man menu once this show was over. Maybe Sophia would benefit from a bit of that herself. She was lovely, but I could tell she was also a bit uptight. A good session in the sack would help loosen her up. I should know. Well, the actual act and afterglow felt amazing. The stress of being 'caught' that went with having a forbidden fling, not so much. In any case, who was I to judge? I barely knew anything about Sophia. We'd only met this evening, so it wasn't for me to say what she should or shouldn't do. I'd crossed enough boundaries with her for one night, so it was best not to pry any further.

Anyway, rather than worrying about Sophia's personal life, I needed to think about what I was going to do to sort out my own. Starting with how I was going to get through another night and day at this exhibition without accidentally falling into bed with Finn.

CHAPTER FOURTEEN

W hat the hell was I thinking, drinking so much last night? I felt like total and utter shit. God knows how I was going to manage spending all day on my feet.

Oh well. It was worth it. I had a laugh with Sophia. She'd be sending the proposal next week, but it was already a done deal in my mind. I was going to enjoy working with her and hopefully having her as a friend too.

I reached for my phone on the mahogany bedside table. It was 6.57 a.m. At least I could spend another half an hour in bed before breakfast arrived. I checked my messages. Finn had asked to come to my room again last night. I was too drunk to send a verbose reply, so I'd just said 'no.' Eventually he'd give up.

I rolled over and pulled the thick white duvet back over my head. As long as I was at the stand for nine-thirty, I should be fine. The hotel was literally opposite the exhibition centre, so I had plenty of time.

Just as I closed my eyes, there was a knock at the door. 'Room service.'

Already? Bollocks. I thought I'd ticked the 7.30 a.m. box.

The door knocked again.

'Room service.'

'Okay, okay. I'm coming!' I said, dragging on the fluffy hotel dressing gown and rubbing my eyes as I opened the door. 'Finn?' I said as he barged inside. Sneaky bastard, putting on a fake voice. 'What are you…'

Before I could finish my sentence, he lifted me up like I was a feather, threw me down on the bed and straddled me.

'I really wish you'd stop ignoring me, Roxy, so I wouldn't have to resort to taking such drastic action. Unless of course you're not interested?' he said cautiously. 'If you genuinely want me to leave, if you're sure you don't want me here, then just say the word and I'll climb off you right now and go.'

I definitely didn't want him to leave. Especially as I remembered how much I'd enjoyed it the last time he'd taken *drastic action* in the stationery cupboard…

'Well, no…I don't *want* you to go. I'd like you to stay right where you are. It's just, I'm worried about—'

He pushed his lips on mine.

'I haven't brushed my teeth!' I cringed.

'Don't care. So,' he said, pulling down his jogging bottoms and revealing his rock-solid rod, which was standing firmly to attention. *Sweet Jesus.* 'Now that I'm here, Roxy, do you want me to fuck you or not?'

'Yes, Finn,' I panted, yanking my dressing gown open, exposing my naked body, knowing that there was nothing that I wanted more. 'Go ahead and fuck me.'

If I thought today might be a struggle before, after that impromptu room service (or should that be a *full-body service*?) from Finn, I knew now that it was *guaranteed* to be a nightmare. But what the hell. That was a banging way to start the morning. *Banging!* I cackled to myself. That was definitely the right word. Pun totally intended. That man was impossible to resist.

By the time we'd shared my breakfast in bed and finished round two, it was almost 8.30 a.m.

'I should really jump in the shower and get dressed,' I groaned, wishing we could just stay here and roll around in bed all day. 'And *you* should get back to your room.'

'Five more minutes…' he said, stroking my face.

'What are we doing, Finn?' I said, sitting up. 'This is crazy. Your mum will go nuts if she finds out.'

'Don't worry about her.'

'Easy for you to say. She thinks the sun shines out of your arse. *I* on the other hand feel like a naughty teenager sneaking around. Colette's already warned me that she'd make mincemeat out of any woman who dares to even look at you.'

'She's always been overprotective with women, but I just ignore her and do what I want anyway. Can't let her control my life.'

If only I could be so blasé about things.

'I know some mums are overprotective, but Colette takes it to a *whole* different level. I don't get why she's like that towards you. Then again, there's loads of things I don't understand about Colette. Like how she was so nice and kind, helping me get away from my ex, yet now she seems so, I don't know, *cold*. I work my butt off for her, but she never acknowledges my efforts. She dumps a load of tasks on me but never says *please* or *thank you*. And she's totally oblivious to my feelings and how she treats me.'

'I know, I know,' he sighed. 'Sadly, that's just Mum. Don't take offense to this, but she's always liked taking on *pet projects* and I think that's how she views you. For as long as I can remember, Mum's liked discovering new talent or helping people "in need". That's why she used to do talks to students, for example. She got a buzz from giving them their first big break.'

'Yeah. That's how we met,' I said. 'When she came to my uni.'

'Right. But once she's *rescued* that person or got them back on their feet, the challenge is over. They kind of lose their "shine" and she loses interest.'

'Charming!' I scoffed.

'It's not personal. Mum also likes to feel wanted. She craves the adoration. The gratitude people show her when she helps them. Not in an arrogant way. More because she needs validation. At work, she's fulfilled. She's busy. She has people that depend on her and look up to her. When she earns a lot of money and the business is doing well, it "proves" that she's worthy. But in her personal life, it's different. She really felt it when I went to the States. Being in that big house all by herself, she got really lonely. She's always relied too much on men. If Mum has a man, then she feels needed. So after the second divorce, and with me thousands of miles away, she felt pretty low. It was hard to get her head round me leaving and another failed marriage. So I think when she saw you again and heard your story, knowing what she'd been through with her recent breakup, on a human level, she wanted to help you avoid the pain she went through. But like I said, I don't think it was entirely selfless.'

'Because I helped her feel validated?'

'Yeah. When Mum invited you to live with her, which was a few months before Donald came along, she needed company. So she wouldn't have to be home alone in the evenings. She knew you'd be grateful, and that would make her feel needed again. So I reckon that now that Donald's on the scene, he's taking her here, there and everywhere, and she's spending so much time with him, she doesn't need you for company anymore. Which means that you're kind of *just an employee*, and so you have to earn your usefulness and your keep at home in other ways.'

'Earn my usefulness! I help the company earn a shed load of money. If I'm *just an employee*, why isn't that enough?'

'I hear what you're saying'—he took a swig of orange juice—'but because you live with her too, she expects more. How can I explain? You know like how when you're a kid at home, you have to do chores like watering the plants or washing up or whatever?'

'Yeah,' I said, thinking back to how Mum used to make me do the dusting and vacuuming every Saturday morning.

'Well, I think Mum asking you to run errands and stuff is the equivalent for her. I know it sounds bad. I could be wrong, but knowing Mum, that's just my take on the situation. The reality is that Donald is the focus of her affections now. All she cares about is her business and him. And me too, I suppose.'

Made sense, although it didn't feel great to hear that I was some sort of pet project, but it had been mutually beneficial in many ways. I supposed Colette got to feel better about herself by taking in a 'charity case' like me, and I got my life back.

'Hmm. Well, whilst that explains a lot, it doesn't excuse her not saying please and thank you occasionally. Surely that's just basic manners. Anyway, it's not just the stuff with your mum that makes this situation complicated. It's also the fact that you're leaving in, what, a week?'

'Pretty much. A week tomorrow. Things needn't be complicated, though. Don't think about the future, Roxy. Let's just enjoy the moment. We'll figure everything out when the time comes.'

Maybe he was right. Maybe I was thinking too much. I just didn't know what to make of it all. On the one hand, I absolutely *didn't* want anything serious. I wanted to play the field. Get out there. Have experiences. With other men. *Why shouldn't I?* I'd wasted so many years withering away, and I didn't want to settle down. But then on the other, the chemistry I had with Finn was off the scale and I wasn't quite ready to completely give up the man who'd given me the best sex I'd ever had.

'Okay,' I sighed. 'Let's just see what happens.'

'Cool. So…I know I just said not to focus on the future, but I was thinking, next weekend, do you want to get a hotel or something?' He sat up straighter and his eyes widened. 'Things would have calmed down at the office for you, so you'll feel more relaxed, and I'll stop working on Friday too, so we can go somewhere and make the most of my last couple of days here?'

Mmm. The prospect of sex on tap with Finn was

appealing. At least then we wouldn't have to worry about Colette. *Seriously.* This was why I needed my own place. I felt like I'd gone back twenty-five years. Never did I think I'd be worrying about getting busted by some guy's mum in my forties. It was embarrassing. I supposed this was the painful reality of starting again with nothing after a divorce. Yes, in the grand scheme of things, it was a million times better than being stuck in a controlling relationship, but still. At this stage of my life, I really shouldn't have to be sneaking around and living like this. Anyway, I couldn't think about moving out just yet, so like I'd said to Alex, I'd just need to keep toeing the line. *For now.*

'Yeah, why not?' I said casually.

'Great! I'll book something. And it doesn't have to be all about sex. We can go out for dinner. Or order in room service, just talk and even watch *Strictly Come Dancing* together. It'll be nice.'

Dinner? Watching TV together? As much as I loved *Strictly*, that was bordering on relationship, boyfriend/girlfriend territory. I didn't want him getting too lovey-dovey. Despite what Finn said, this situation was already complicated. *Can't muddy the waters more by catching feelings.*

Finn jumped up and kissed me on my forehead. 'Anyway, I'd better go and get ready. And, Roxy?'

'Finn?'

'Please don't ignore me today. It's very annoying, and I know you think you're doing the right thing and that it will put me off, but it actually makes me want you even more. *Just saying…*'

'I'll try my best,' I smirked.

So much for avoiding Finn and staying out of trouble. I was already looking forward to our dirty weekend…

In just a week, he'd be gone and these sex sessions would be a distant memory. So I'd decided that I was going to enjoy this forbidden fling.

Yes. Rather than thinking about what might or might not happen, I was going to take Finn's advice and start living well and truly in the moment.

CHAPTER FIFTEEN

'Success!' Colette smiled. 'We have sold out of literally all of the stock we bought, and the pictures the magazine's photographer took of me with the editor for the prize draw earlier looked wonderful! I told you that you could pull it off.'

'Well, it wasn't just me. The team have all worked so hard, and of course Finn has been a great help,' I said, pushing a flashback of his mouth all over my body earlier this morning out of my mind and trying to focus.

'Yes, I'm very proud of my son. And I have to say, I'm very relieved that he's back to his normal self today. Last night he was snappy again. But today, he was all smiles. I asked him at dinner if he'd spoken to that Ruth, and he assured me he hadn't, so I was starting to think that maybe he was taking drugs or something because of all of his mood swings these past few days. I was extremely worried this morning when I knocked on his door to ask him if he wanted to come down to breakfast with me and there was no answer.'

'Probably just in bed…' I said, thinking that at least I was saying something that was actually true. There was no need to clarify whose bed I was referring to…

'Well, I couldn't be sure,' replied Colette. 'Like I said, he was incredibly miserable last night, so when I kept knocking loudly and he didn't come to the door and then he didn't answer his mobile or the phone in his room, I thought, what if he's taken an overdose or something? That's when I knew I had to get in there.'

Is she having a laugh?

'What? You let yourself into his room?'

'Well, yes. When we arrived at the hotel, I checked in with him, and whilst he'd gone to the gents, I asked the receptionist for a spare key. *I'm his mother*. I needed to know that he was okay.'

'Jesus, Colette! You treat him like a five-year-old!'

Oh shit. Did I just say that out loud?

Colette looked like I'd just punched her in the face. She was wounded. Hurt. Shocked. I hadn't meant for it to come out so bluntly. In fact, it wasn't supposed to come out of my mouth at all, *but seriously*. Didn't she see how overprotective and crazy she was? So Finn didn't answer his door or his phone. *Big deal!* Rather than thinking he could be in the shower, taking a dump, sleeping or that he'd gone for a run, she'd automatically thought the worst. I mean, I got the whole mood swings thing and why she might be a little concerned, but Finn was probably one of the *least* likely people I knew to take drugs. He didn't smoke, ate healthily, kept his body in shape and was very level-headed. I know you can't always tell because some people are good at hiding these things, but it wasn't like he'd been missing or unreachable for hours or anything. *Jeez.*

'Sorry, Colette, I didn't mean to snap.' I softened my voice, hoping my mini-outburst wouldn't get me in hot water. 'It's just, there's a million causes for mood swings. And I don't think, in Finn's case, taking an illegal substance is one of them.'

'Yes. That tone was a little uncalled for.' She frowned. 'I hope you're right, though, Roxy. He's my one and only child, and I couldn't bear the thought of losing him,' she sighed. I glanced down at the floor, not knowing what else to say. *Well, this is awkward.* 'Anyway!' she said, clapping her hands to indicate a change of subject. *Thank goodness.* 'He seems okay. That's the main thing. I'll just need to keep a closer eye on him.' *Any closer and you'll lose your head up his backside.* 'Let's get going. The team can take care of the packing up. Once Finn gets back from the van, we'll get a cab to the station and take the train to London. You can either head off whenever you're ready or wait and get the train back with us,' replied Colette.

That's a hard no. I'd definitely rather travel solo. Could you imagine a two-hour journey with them? I politely declined, went and said my goodbyes to the team, got my overnight bag from the hotel, then jumped in a taxi to Manchester Piccadilly station.

Just as the train pulled into London Euston, my phone rang.

'Hi, Roxy,'

'Hi, Colette, everything okay?' I asked. This paranoia

was getting ridiculous. Literally every time she wanted to speak to me, I was convinced that she knew. It was silly, really, because if she did, there was no way she'd be so calm. Everything was tickety-boo.

'Yes, all good, thanks. We're on the train. Should get to London in about an hour. I was just talking to Finn, and he made me see that perhaps I have been overworking you. I know I've expected a lot with organising the exhibition and everything single-handed, and I should show my appreciation a little more, so although I know it's not much, why don't I start by giving you the day off tomorrow? Let you have some time to recuperate.'

Wonders will never cease.

'That would be great, thank you,' I said, thinking how desperate I was to catch up on my sleep. After our conversation this morning, Finn must have decided he'd stick up for me and tell Colette some home truths about her behaviour. So sweet of him to fight my corner.

'That's settled, then. I think I'll take the day off too. Donald's invited me over tonight. We made up on the phone last night, so I'm looking forward to seeing him. I'll drop Finn off in the cab and then head straight over there. And thinking ahead to Saturday, maybe we could all have a lovely lunch together? My treat. Perhaps go out somewhere nice. Will you be around?'

Dammit. There go the hotel plans.

'Glad to hear you've patched things up with Donald,' I said, stepping off the train. 'Erm, as for Saturday, I'm not sure. I'd already planned to go somewhere. Can I let you know later this week?'

'Sure. Well, I hope you can join us. I've got to make the most of my time with Finn before he leaves,' she said.

My sentiments exactly.

'I understand,' I replied. 'Well, enjoy your night with Donald.'

'Thanks, Roxy. I will. Thanks again for your hard work.'

Wow. She'd actually said *thank you*. Twice. Finn had worked some serious magic.

Oooh, I said to myself. If Colette was going to Donald's tonight, then that meant…

My phone pinged. I clicked on the message.

Finn

Looks like we've got the place to ourselves tonight… I'll text when we're in the cab.

Finn

Getting hard thinking about the things I'd like us to do together. Be ready for me…

Me

You better get some sleep whilst you're on the train, because you're going to need the energy…

Finn

Don't worry, Rox…As always, this Energizer Bunny is ready to go all night…

Oh yes. That's what I like to hear. Looked like he'd Googled the Energizer Bunny too...

As I jumped in a black cab, excitement shot through me like lightning. I couldn't wait to see Finn. To *feel* him. At least I didn't have to hold on for too much longer. If he was about an hour behind, that should give me enough time to shower and slip into something that was sure to get him going...

'Hello, sexy,' said Finn, stepping into the hallway, kicking the door behind him and dropping his bag on the floor.

'Hello *yourself*,' I said, casually walking towards him. I was wearing a short burgundy leather dress. Hopefully I wouldn't have it on for much longer...

Finn rushed towards me, pulled me in for a kiss and slid his hand up the front of my dress.

'Mmm...no underwear. *Nice.*'

'Didn't want you to waste valuable time taking it off...'

'Thank you,' he said, stroking me. 'I cannot wait to fuck you. So glad we've got the place to ourselves.'

'I know,' I said, unbuckling his brown leather belt. 'But we can't mess things up like last time. No leaving our clothes in the kitchen, screwing on the dining table or dropping wine over the carpet. And we need to make sure we're back in our own beds by tomorrow morning. Can't risk getting caught.'

'You worry too much,' he said, nibbling on my neck. 'You need to relax, and I know exactly how to help you do that...'

Finn and I started kissing like we were competing in a snogathon. Our hands were everywhere. Before I knew it, he'd gently pushed me down against the cold marble staircase.

'Let's go up to my room,' I panted.

'No, I can't wait. I'm going to do you right here,' he said as he knelt down, yanked up my dress, spread my legs and then buried his head in between them.

Oh God.

I grabbed his head and pushed it in deeper. *Hell yeah.*

'Yes…right there,' I commanded as his tongue flicked up and down.

I closed my eyes, and my body felt like it was about to explode. I ran my hand underneath his shirt and dug my nails into his back.

Finn was right. I worried too much. Well, not tonight. Not for the next twelve hours. I was going to enjoy every single second.

I pulled down his trousers and then his boxers, exposing his beautiful naked arse. I gripped his butt cheek with one hand and wrapped my hand around his solid rod with the other. *Jesus.* I couldn't wait to feel him inside me. But I wasn't quite ready for him to stop what he was doing yet…

Just as Finn's tongue began circling my clit I heard a scream. I opened my eyes to see Colette standing at the front door, her mouth on the floor.

'What the hell are you doing?!' she shouted. Finn spun his head around. 'Aaaaargghhh! Oh my God! Oh my God!' Colette was jumping up and down like a madwoman. Her eyes were bulging from her head. 'What are you…? Get your filthy vagina away from my son's mouth, you disgusting whore!'

'Shit,' said Finn, quickly wiping his mouth and pulling up his boxers. 'Look, Mum, it's—'

Just as I yanked down my dress to cover my modesty, Colette screamed again and charged at me like a bull.

Finn jumped in front of me and held his arms out to stop her.

'Mum, just calm down,' he shouted. 'Don't you dare touch her!'

'Calm down? Calm down?' she said, trying to push past him. 'How could you, Roxy? *How could you?'* she screamed, covering her eyes as if she was trying to erase the last minute from her brain. 'He's my son, Roxy. *My little boy*. And you…you've corrupted him. Taken advantage of him. Made him do those things to you. You're practically old enough to be his mother. It's disgusting! *Disgusting!'*

'Enough!' shouted Finn. 'I'm sick and tired of you treating me like a child. How many times do I have to tell you? I'm not your little boy any more. I'm a grown man. Roxy didn't *make me* do anything. I was the one that pursued her. *I* wanted to fuck *her*.'

'Finn!' said Colette, taking a step back. 'Watch your mouth! What's got into you?'

'Nothing has got into me. I'm a man, Mother. I grew up a long time ago. I lost my virginity when I was seventeen, for God's sake. And as hard as it may be for you to hear, I have been having sex ever since. And I like it. *A lot.* Especially with Roxy.'

'This is…this is *hideous*…!' said Colette, covering her ears and then pacing up and down. 'I can't believe what

I'm hearing. This is just…this is too much!' She charged at me again, and Finn held her back once more. 'I *trusted* you, Roxy. I asked you to look after him. I told you to keep those floozies away from him, and look what you've done! Turned him into a potty-mouthed commoner like you!' She ducked under Finn's arm and charged at me, then slapped me round the face. *Fuck. That hurt.*

Finn lifted Colette away as her legs dangled in the air.

'I can't believe you would do this to me after all I've done for you. Gave you a home and a job and this is how you repay me? By *betraying* me? I had a feeling that something wasn't right. And there I was thinking it was that Ruth or drugs. Not realising that it was ten times worse! How long has this been going on? Actually, no. I don't want to know. Imagine if I hadn't realised I didn't pack enough of my tablets and asked the taxi driver to turn back. You would have had your filthy, hussy hands all over him. Well, not any more. It's over! I want you out of this house. And you can forget about coming back to work. You're fired!'

I felt tears pricking in my eyes. I was rooted to the spot. *In shock.* Don't know why, really, when I knew this would bloody happen. I *knew* I was playing with fire, yet I carried on. It *was* my fault. No point me trying to say otherwise. Colette was right. I should've steered clear of Finn. But I hadn't, and now I was going to suffer the consequences.

'I'm sorry, Colette,' I said softly as Finn held on to her tightly to stop her launching at me again. 'I'll go and pack my things, then I'll leave.'

'No, you won't! Here,' she said, breaking free from Finn, picking up my coat from the stand, grabbing my handbag and boots from the floor, then thrusting them into my arms. 'You'll go *right now*. *I'll* pack up your things and send them to you, or you can collect them next week once Finn's gone.'

'Fine.' I said as I walked towards the front door.

'Roxy, no!' said Finn, grabbing my arm. 'Don't go! I want you to stay. I *need* you to stay. I think I'm falling in love with you…'

He's what?

I paused, then turned back. I looked in his eyes. He meant it.

Bloody hell.

Yeah, I had feelings for Finn. *Lustful* feelings. My body couldn't get enough of him. But *love*? That was some deep shit. *Yes.* We had mind-blowing sex, but it could never be more than that. Like he'd just said, we fucked, we didn't *make love*. Finn was about to start a new job and had a life in LA. I lived here. In London. And as much as I liked being with him, I was still finding myself, trying to build my own life, and I wasn't ready for anything serious.

Even if I *did* decide to continue seeing him, just think of all the shit it would stir up. I looked at Colette and saw the horror and hatred in her eyes. I'd never seen her look at me or *anyone* like that before. To say she was pissed off would be the understatement of the century. The threats she'd made before certainly wouldn't stay empty. That was the face of a woman who wanted to draw blood.

Staying with Finn would mess up my life. Was I willing to throw away everything I'd worked for over a man? Just for great sex? Even though it looked like I was already screwed, that was no reason to make things worse.

Didn't matter how good Finn was in the sack—I wasn't his pimp, so his dick wasn't going to pay the bills.

No. This wouldn't work.

'I'm sorry, Finn,' I said, kissing him gently on the cheek, then stepping towards the door. 'I've got to go. I think you're amazing. I'll always remember the time we spent together, but you need to forget about me. You're going back to LA in a week, you're about to start a brilliant new job, and you've got your whole life ahead of you. Go and enjoy it.'

'But, Roxy…!' I couldn't stay to hear what he said. I rushed outside, clutching my boots, coat and handbag, and started running barefoot, out of the driveway, then down the street. Running, running and running.

I had no idea where I was going. All I knew was that after my divorce, I'd had a second chance at life. A fresh start. I was given a place to stay. I had a job that I loved. Just over a week ago, things were going great. I had the world at my feet, but I'd tossed it down the toilet. All because I couldn't keep my legs closed. *Unbelievable.*

How could I be so bloody stupid? And most importantly, what the hell was I going to do now?

CHAPTER SIXTEEN

I t had now been just over a week since that shitty Sunday night when my whole world had come crashing down.

Since then, Alex had been an absolute diamond, letting me stay with her. But she only had a small house, and as grateful as I was to have a roof over my head, her sofa was doing my back in. Can't say listening to her screaming her head off whenever she brought home one of her Tinder dates was much fun either. Still, at least by the sounds of it, she was enjoying herself.

Getting an insight into the whole dating thing was a bit of an eye opener. Alex would tell me she was meeting a guy for a drink and I'd get excited about having the place to myself, but then it barely seemed like she'd been gone an hour or two before they'd come bursting through her front door and into her room and the bedroom gymnastics would begin.

I noticed that the guys never stayed the night, which always upset Alex, but at least that way there weren't any feelings involved. Both parties could just get what they wanted without having to worry about controlling mothers sticking their oar in, expectations of entering a serious relationship, losing their jobs and completely fucking up their lives like I'd done with that Finn fling.

Every time I thought about how I'd screwed things up, it just made me want to pull the duvet back over my head. *So sodding stupid.*

I should be at work right now. Not sitting here in my PJs watching daytime TV. I had loads of great leads from the exhibition. Lots of potential customers that I'd promised to call. Now they probably thought I was some unreliable bullshitter. I'd emailed Colette a list of contacts, but she hadn't replied, so who knew if she'd do anything with it?

I bloody loved that job. Even though it was hard work, it challenged me. There was room to grow. The company was going from strength to strength. After the exhibition, I had gotten the feeling that we were on the cusp of something big. I keep saying *we*, but it wasn't *we* anymore, was it? It was *them*. I was no longer part of the team. I reckoned the company's success would be huge. Especially with Sophia and her PR team on board. And now I was going to miss out on all of that. All that hard work, all those late nights, had been flushed straight down the toilet.

It had hurt so much when I'd had to call Sophia and tell her I'd left the company, so wasn't sure if the project would still go ahead. She'd asked me what had happened, but unlike the first night we'd met, this time I'd managed to keep my big mouth shut. Slagging off my ex was one thing, but telling her I'd been sacked after the boss had walked in on her son going down on me in her hallway would definitely tip the scale of unprofessionalism.

I said that Sophia was still welcome to contact Colette and pitch to her—after all, the company shouldn't suffer because I couldn't keep my knickers on—but Sophia said she'd hold off for now and suggested we keep in touch.

Maybe she was waiting to see what company I'd go and work at next. *Pff.* I wouldn't hold my breath if I was her. My name was probably mud in the industry now. Colette had no doubt begun her revenge campaign against me. She'd probably already sent out an email blast saying:

Do not hire this whore if you have a son or male family members in their twenties. This shameless cougar will corrupt and have her wicked way with them. Beware.

If I really wanted to shag a younger man, I should have just found one on a dating app. What's that saying? *Don't shit where you eat.* Oh and then there's: *don't bite the hand that feeds you.* And of course: *don't shit in your own back-yard.* There's a million ways to express it which all mean the same thing. Don't fuck your boss's son. I knew this, but what did I do? Went and took a big fat dump not just in the backyard, but all over my life.

There was no way I was going to get a job now. I'd only been at Cole Beauty Solutions for around ten months, and before that I had an eleven-year gap on my CV. That wasn't going to help me secure a job at the same level. Even if I got to the interview stage, and even if by some miracle they offered me a job, it would be curtains for me. They'd want a reference, wouldn't they? And given that Colette had last described me as a potty-mouthed commoner and filthy hussy, I didn't think they'd be queuing up round the block to hire me.

Yep. Things were looking pretty crappy on the job front. Same on the flat-hunting front too. I'd thought the prices were high when I rented a place straight after leaving Steve, but they'd shot up even more since then. I'd worked so hard to save whilst I was staying at Colette's, and now I was going to blow it all on rent when I could have been putting that down as a deposit for my first proper home.

I also had to pay for storage. Basically, Colette had texted me on Wednesday morning to say she'd packed up my things and that if I called round, Jean the cleaner would open the door for me to collect them. I'd had to hire a man with a van to take it all.

When I'd moved in with Colette, I'd brought along the bed, wardrobe and a few other bits I'd bought when I first lived on my own, and she'd let me keep them in one of her spare rooms. After the painful hours I'd spent putting together that stuff from IKEA, there was no way I could throw it all away, and it definitely wouldn't fit in Alex's house. Which meant I'd have to have them stored elsewhere. Yet another expense. *Entirely my own fault. Should have kept away from her son.*

Yes. Finn. After I'd left that night, he'd called and texted so many times asking to talk. He'd even messaged Alex, asking if she'd speak to me. If he'd found out where she lived, he probably would have come here to find me.

It was hard. I *did* want to speak to him. Say a proper goodbye. But everything was already such a mess and I didn't want to make it worse. Plus, knowing that he'd started catching feelings, I figured that it would be better for him if we cut all contact. The sooner we stopped talking, the sooner he'd get over me and I'd forget about him.

Easier said than done. I still found myself thinking about him. Sex with Finn was *amazing*. But getting my leg over with him had cost me so much. Now that I thought about it, I would have been better off hiring an escort. In fact, it would have been better altogether if I'd never met Finn at all.

CHAPTER SEVENTEEN

'Rox, you know I love you, right?' said Alex as she sat down beside me on her sofa.

'I sense there's a *but* coming…?' I replied nervously.

'*But*, I think it's time that you sorted yourself out. It's been almost two weeks now. You should be getting yourself out there. Finding another job or at least looking at flats…'

'I'm getting under your feet, aren't I?' I winced.

'Well…it's just that I'm used to having things a certain way, you know? Not having the dishes stacking up for days on end or having the living room look like a tip…'

'Sorry. I was always really tidy at Colette's. I always washed up my stuff and kept my room tidy. It's just—I guess I haven't been able to find the motivation to do *anything*.'

'Have you forgotten who you are?' She folded her arms. 'What you've been through? What you've achieved? You found the courage to walk away from your dickhead husband, started a job, which you're bloody brilliant at by the way, and built up your confidence. And what, just because you pissed off your boss and she kicked you out, you're going to give up? Just like that? That's not the Roxy I used to know. The Roxy I love would say: *big fat giant bollocks to that*. She'd say *screw Colette*. *Fuck wallowing and feeling sorry for myself*. She'd jump off that sofa, and she'd go and knock on every door until she got another job. She'd find herself a flat again, make it as nice as she could whilst she carried on saving for her dream home. The *real* Roxy would also get out there and continue exploring the saucy side of her personality that Finn helped her to discover, by getting on those apps and having some fun.'

'I just don't know if I'm strong enough to start all over again,' I said, hanging my head. 'I thought after the last time, that would be it. It was *so* hard before. I can't face starting from zero again. I've got nothing.'

'What's wrong with you?' She slapped her forehead. 'Did you not listen to anything I just said? You're *not* starting from zero. You were before, yes, but not now. You've got confidence. Self-belief. You didn't have that before, and although it seems to have taken a mini-break right now, it's still within you. You just have to drag it out. You've got, what, almost a year of experience that you didn't have before. You've got contacts. Loads of them. Do you know how many brands would *kill* to have someone like you on their team? Colette's competitors, for starters. I know we're related, but I've been doing my job for years, and I've never met someone who has learnt the ropes so quickly and done as well as you. You were practi-cally managing a whole department and a national sales force single-handedly. Most companies have *multiple* people to do your job.'

'Yeah, you're right about that,' I sighed. 'I told Colette it was too much and that I needed help.'

'Exactly. You're worth much more to her than you realise.'

'Well, clearly not. Otherwise she wouldn't have fired me. Maybe you're right about getting myself back out there, though, and finding a job. I can't go back to that couch potato lifestyle again. I won't contact Colette's competitors, though. It wouldn't be right.'

I knew I shouldn't be worrying about staying loyal to her after she'd chucked me out in the street without giving my well-being a second thought, but I couldn't help it. Despite everything, she'd still done a lot for me and I couldn't ever forget that.

'Fair enough,' said Alex. 'I probably wouldn't be able to do something like that either. All I'm saying is that you have options. A lot more than you think.'

I looked around the living room. There were empty boxes of Pringles, a bottle of gin, empty cans of tonic strewn over the floor and half-eaten Chinese takeaway containers from last night on the coffee table. On the TV, an episode of some awful tabloid talk show had just started with the title: *My husband is addicted to using blow-up dolls.*

Dear God.

I hadn't left the house for days. I felt like shit and I didn't even need a mirror to know that I looked like shit.

I sniffed my armpits. *Jeez.* And I *definitely* needed to take a shower.

This was ridiculous. Was *this* really how I wanted to

spend my days? Had I gone through hell after Steve to let a little setback defeat me?

Hell no.

'Fuck it,' I said, jumping off the sofa. 'I'm going in the bathroom to give myself a good wash. After that I'll tidy up this room, which looks like a bunch of slobs have been camping out here for years, and then I'm going to get online, set up some flat viewings, sort out my CV, then make some calls. It's time to get my shit together and get my life back on track.'

It'd been a week since I'd moved into my flat. It wasn't much, just a small one-bed with a little open-plan living room and kitchen and a teeny bathroom, but it was mine. I had my own space again and could live by my own rules. And as I had my deposit ready to go and could move in straight away (and probably because the landlord was desperate), I'd even gotten a sweet deal on the rent, so it cost a little bit less than the market rate. Which meant I wouldn't be eating into my savings as much as I feared. And I'd get another job again soon. I was sure of it.

When I thought about it, I *did* have a lot to offer. I'd achieved loads in the short space of time that I'd been at that company. Like Alex said, I'd done the job of multiple people. Run a whole department. I knew a lot about the industry. By rights, they should be biting my hand off.

That day that Alex had given me a talking-to and made me see sense, I'd made some calls to some contacts and to a couple of recruitment agencies and managed to line up interviews pretty quickly. I'd been to a few already, but none of them had felt right. Whilst the money was good, they were either too corporate and stuffy, which just isn't my style, or didn't give me enough autonomy. That was what I'd loved about my job at Cole Beauty Solutions. Yes, Colette might have piled on the work, but at least she'd trusted me to get on with it. She'd listened to my ideas, and there hadn't been a hundred layers of management to go through to get something approved. If it made sense, was a reasonable cost and was going to make her money, get more customers or help the company grow, then generally she would support it.

And I'd liked the fact that there were opportunities for promotion. Whilst Colette wasn't really one to praise, I reckoned that if I was still there, it wouldn't be long until I was made a director. Who knows? One day, she might have even asked me to run the whole business, so she could sail off into the sunset with Donald. Not sure if I'd want to take on that level of responsibility, but at least there was maybe an option there in the future if I did. Anyway, pointless thinking about that now. I'd find another job. But I wasn't going to rush into anything or take something out of desperation. I knew my worth now, and my future employer would need to recognise that too.

Believe it or not, in between all the job-hunting and sorting out my new flat, I'd even found time to get on the apps. I'd hooked up with a guy last night. It wasn't anything to write home about. He couldn't even begin to compare to Finn, but he was nice enough. Thirty-one, okay looking, okay body. Not sure if I'd see him again. I'd been feeling so shitty these past few weeks that I'd needed to de-stress, and he had given me the release that I'd needed, so mission accomplished on that front at least.

I think he probably would have stayed the night if I'd let him, but I wanted my own space. I had a lot that I wanted to get done today and knew I needed a good night's sleep. Now that I was motivated again, I didn't want any man, anyone or anything getting in my way.

Today I'd already been to IKEA to pick up a few more bits, collected my dry cleaning for an interview at a hair tools company on Monday, fired off my CV to a few more people, and later tonight I'd probably relax with a glass of wine and see if I could set up some more dates for this weekend. But first, I needed to get some food in, as the cupboards were bare.

As I stepped into the supermarket, I started to make a mental list of what I needed. Bread, milk, couple of bottles of wine…oh, and I'd pick up some fresh flowers too. Help brighten up the flat.

I started heading over to look at a pretty bunch that caught my eye, but then I froze.

Standing less than ten feet away, it was her. Sniffing a bouquet of roses. The woman that hated my guts. Who'd called me a filthy whore.

It's Colette.

Fuck.

CHAPTER EIGHTEEN

At first I'd thought about hiding, turning around and running away. But then I thought, *no*. Why should I? I'd done a lot of thinking and soul-searching over the past week, and do you know what? Whilst sleeping with the boss's son wasn't my finest moment, I wasn't ashamed of it.

Finn was right. Sometimes we're attracted to people and we can't help how we feel. I'd tried to fight it. *So hard.* I really had, but ultimately it was too strong. And anyway, in the grand scheme of things, it was hardly the crime of the century. I hadn't murdered anyone, for God's sake. I hadn't forced myself on him. He was a willing participant. *More than willing.* He'd chased me. Yes, I could have said no, but ultimately I hadn't wanted to. And you know what else? I didn't regret meeting him. I didn't regret fucking him. I'd never felt more alive. He'd helped me to become more confident in the bedroom. Ask for what I wanted. He'd given me feelings I'd never felt before.

Finn had helped me believe in myself more. Yeah, my confidence had grown before I'd met him, but up until that point, I'd kind of felt a bit ashamed that I was attracted to younger men and thought that they wouldn't be interested in me. But my fling with Finn had shown me that a woman's sex appeal doesn't stop once we hit our thirties or forties. We *can* still be desirable to men of *all* ages.

It's crazy. Women are constantly judged if they date someone younger, whilst men are given a pat on the back for doing the same thing. But I did some reading on it, and actually women's attraction to younger guys makes a lot of sense because ladies hit their sexual prime in their thirties and forties, whereas men reach it in their twenties. And because they have more stamina, for someone like me who is just looking for fun, it's often an ideal match.

Now, because of my experience with Finn, if I was attracted to a man, whether he was thirty-five or twenty-five, I wasn't going to give a toss about what people thought. At the end of the day, it was my life and my body. From now on, I wasn't answering to anyone but myself. So if Colette wanted to charge at me and start hurling insults in the middle of the supermarket, then so be it. I was done trying to impress her and seek her approval. I wanted some flowers for my flat and whether she was standing there or not, I was going to go ahead and choose them, goddammit.

As I approached the display, Colette looked up and the blood literally drained from her face. I continued walking and Sod's Law, the very bouquet I wanted just happened to be right in front of her.

Oh well. Too bad.

'He—hello, Roxy,' Colette said. Her voice was much

softer than I expected. It kind of freaked me out a little. 'How have you been?'

WTF?

Finn's acronyms had started to rub off on me.

Did she actually ask me how I'd been? I must be hallu-cinating. Either that or she was being nice to me so I'd let down my guard and then she'd punch me in the face.

'Fine, thanks,' I said robotically.

'Glad to hear it,' she replied, taking a step towards me.

Here we go. Any minute now she was going to whack me one. Well, she could give it her best shot. But she better know that if she hit me, I'd hit her back.

'I was going to call you, actually…'

'What?' I frowned. Why? Were there some insults that she'd forgotten to hurl at me the last time? Had she since studied a thesaurus and found some other words for whore? *Tart? Slapper? Tramp?* Well, if she wanted to try and call me any of those, then I was ready for her, because I was neither. I was just a woman who had a connection with another consenting man. That was it. *End of.*

'I wanted to apologise. For the things I said. The way I treated you.'

She wants to what? Apologise? My jaw fell to the floor.

'Look, I know I'm probably the last person you want to speak to right now, but do you have ten minutes to go for a coffee? Right here—just in the supermarket café? There's some things I want to tell you. That I'd like to explain.'

I was not expecting this. *At all.* Should I listen to her? She had said some pretty crappy things. I wasn't sure. Then again, if I thought of the bigger picture, if she was feeling guilty, she might be more likely to give me a good reference. And also, I was a little intrigued to know what had caused this change of heart. I supposed ten minutes wouldn't hurt.

'Ten minutes,' I said sternly. 'I've got plans for this evening, and I've still got to do my shopping, so…'

'Wonderful!' Her face brightened. 'Thank you, Roxy. I promise, ten minutes. Just let me pay for these items quickly.'

We sat down at a wooden table for two, and I waited for her to speak.

'So, like I said, I was going to call you, to apologise and to ask you if you want to come back. To work at the company.'

What the actual…? Just like that? *So she says sorry, offers me a job and then I'm just supposed to say yes?* I bet she expected me to bend down and kiss her feet too whilst I was at it.

And it was all a bit fishy to me. Why the sudden change? She'd probably tried to hire someone to do my job and they'd laughed in her face when they'd heard what she expected them to do for that salary. So now she wanted to get me back in again as cheap labour. As much as I'd loved the job, I wasn't going to be her skivvy again. She could forget it.

'Thanks, but no thanks.'

'What?' Her face fell. 'But you *love* that job. I know you do? You *must* come back. You simply *have* to!'

Now she sounded desperate. Was there more to this?

'I'm curious, though…' I rested my finger on my chin. 'What's brought on this U-turn? Why do I *have to*? Is all the work stacking up?'

'Well, yes, but, no. It's just that…*Finn*. He won't talk to me. He won't forgive me unless…'

'Unless?'

'Unless…I make amends with you,' she said, hanging her head.

'I think you'd better explain, Colette.'

'Well, after you left that night—'

'You mean, after you kicked me out and called me a whore?' I snapped.

'Well, yes, once again, I'm very sorry about that. After I hastily asked you to leave, Finn packed his stuff and left. I don't know where he stayed. I assumed maybe he'd caught up with you or something, but later I found out he hadn't. I even waited at the airport to catch him before his flight, but he ignored me. He wouldn't take my calls. I was worried sick, so last week I couldn't take it anymore. I had to see him, to speak to him. So I flew to LA. When I finally got to see him, we had a terrible argument. It was awful, but we got everything out of our systems. He was furious. Said I smothered him. Treated him like a child. Then I told him what had happened to make me this way.'

'Which is…?' I folded my arms.

'It's still hard to talk about. As you know, Finn is my only child. My only *living* child. The thing is, I had another child. Before Finn. I miscarried, almost five months into my pregnancy. It was a boy. I was so excited. I couldn't wait for my firstborn. And then I lost him. I was devastated. Blamed myself. Told myself I'd done something wrong. That if I'd taken better care of my sweet baby boy growing inside of me, he would have survived. It almost destroyed me.' She reached into her handbag, took out a tissue and wiped away the tears that had started to roll down her cheeks.

'So when I got pregnant again a year later, with Finn, I was completely ridden with fear. I was excited, of course, but also terrified that it would happen again. I worried throughout my pregnancy, which of course wasn't good. And then when he was born, I was always paranoid that something would happen to him. He was my little miracle and I had to protect him at all costs. I tried to have more children but struggled to fall pregnant again, and ultimately that stress and the pressure I put on myself led to arguments and the breakdown of my marriage with Finn's dad, who left me. Then it was just me and Finn, and I suppose I became even more protective, and well...so that's why I am the way I am.' She sniffed.

Shit. I had no idea. Colette had never told me about all of that. She'd always been a bit cagey about why she'd divorced her first husband. Now I knew why. You could tell just talking about this was still heartbreaking for her. It still seemed so raw.

'I'm so sorry to hear about what happened to you. But I'm sure it was nothing to do with anything you'd done. You shouldn't have blamed yourself.'

'I know. I realise now that it wasn't my fault, but at the time, I was grieving so much, I suppose I wasn't thinking rationally. And when Finn was born, I was just so relieved. *So happy.* I fell in love with him straight away. I adored him. He was my world. Such a loving boy when he was younger. I guess I just wanted him to stay that way forever. So that I could feel needed. Wanted and loved. I know it's sad, but he's all I've got, Roxy. I can't lose him. That's why I need you to come back.' She rested her hands on top of mine.

'So what exactly were Finn's conditions for making amends with me?'

'Well'—she moved her hands and reached for a fresh tissue—'when Finn said his piece, I apologised and promised I would do anything to make it up to him, to show that I was serious about treating him like an adult and committed to changing. So he told me he'd only talk to me again if I apologised to you and gave you your job back. He said *he'd* pursued *you* and you turned him down so many times because you didn't want to betray me. He insisted that you'd tried to do the right thing, but he hadn't let up. And he told me you were the best thing that's ever happened to the company. He said once I'd done those two things, then I could get back in touch with him and we'd take things from there.'

Unbelievable.

'So basically'—I crossed my arms—'Finn blackmailed you into apologising and giving me my job back? The only reason you're talking to me is because you want to speak to him? Well,' I said, standing up to leave, 'you can forget it. As nice as it is for Finn to say those things, I don't want a job because *he* realises what I bring to the company. I want *you* to realise what I have to offer. I want *you* to want to offer me the job, but not to do it because he's twisted your arm. Goodbye, Colette.'

'Roxy! Wait!' she shouted. I turned around. 'But I *do* want you back. I miss you. The whole team does, and our customers. I *do* realise how valuable you are.'

'Prove it,' I said, putting my hands on my hips.

'How? What do you mean?'

'Show me that you're serious. That you *really* appreciate me. Go away and think about a package that you'd like to offer me and a role with a more reasonable workload, and then call me and I'll *consider* it.' Colette's mouth was on the floor. I had never spoken up for myself to her before, and you could tell she wasn't expecting it.

'Look, Colette. I know you weren't happy about me sleeping with Finn, but I don't regret what happened. I always did my job and what was needed of me. I always delivered. Above and beyond. Finn's a great guy and we enjoyed each other's company, so I can't apologise for that. You just need to get over it. I've told you so many times how grateful I am for everything that you've done for me. But I can't be controlled again. I *won't*.'

That was the other thing I'd realised. Alex was right. By allowing Colette to dictate who I shouldn't sleep with and by giving into all of her demands, I was repeating the same pattern that I'd fallen into with Steve. Back then, I'd thought because I'd left Steve, I'd finally regained full control, but I hadn't come as far as I'd initially thought. The type of control she had over me might have been different, and unlike Steve, I don't think Colette was doing it deliberately or maliciously, but the result was effectively the same. I was giving someone else power over my life and the decisions I made. Always putting their needs before mine. But all of that ended now.

'I won't have someone telling me how to live my life,' I continued. 'I won't pander to your unreasonable requests. And I'm not prepared to be overworked and taken for granted again. If you think you can deal with that, Colette, then *be a darling* and let me know what you've got in mind and I'll think about it. If not, I have *lots* of interviews lined up next week and I'm sure one of those MDs will see what I can bring to the table and make me an offer I can't refuse. Anyway, I'm leaving. Enjoy your weekend.'

I strutted out of the café with my head held high. I couldn't believe I'd said all of that! I'd never have had the confidence to do that before. I'd become too dependent on Colette. Our lives were too intertwined. Relying on her for both a place to live and a job was too much. It had made me too scared to do or say the wrong thing. I saw that now. But *no more*. As well as finding my voice in my personal life, I'd also finally found my professional voice. I knew my worth, and I wasn't going to settle for anything less.

CHAPTER NINETEEN

It was Saturday afternoon and I was knackered after finishing my first full week back at Cole Beauty Solutions.

Yes. I'd returned.

Colette had come good. She'd made me an offer I would have been stupid to turn down. I'd still let her stew for a day before accepting, though. Didn't want her to think I was desperate.

As well as an assistant and my own office, Colette had also given me a whopper of a pay rise. I'd nearly collapsed when I'd read the email. My first thought was, *Holy shit! Is she serious? That's a* lot *of money.* But then I'd channelled my inner Beyoncé and reminded myself that I was worth every penny.

What were my thoughts after five full working days back there? I'd say, *so far, so good.* Colette was a lot more appreciative of the work I was doing and praised me constantly. At times it was a little OTT, but she was trying, and that meant a lot.

Luckily the leads I had from the show were still warm when I'd started following up, and fingers crossed, they'd result in loads of new customers for our company. Yep. Now that I was back on the team, I could start saying *our* and *we* again.

Colette had also approved the appointment of Sophia's firm to manage the PR for the upcoming launch, so they'd be starting in two weeks' time and I was really looking forward to it. I'd met up for lunch with Sophia on Thursday near her office and we'd got on like a house on fire again. Hopefully, when things were a bit calmer for her at work, we could meet up socially on a weekend or one evening too.

Things were also coming along nicely with my flat. It was starting to feel more like home. Colette had offered me my old room back at her house. Whilst it would mean I wouldn't have to shell out a big chunk of my salary on rent, I'd said no because I wanted to stand on my own two feet. That was really important to me. You can't put a price on independence. Anyway, with my pretty pay rise and the rest of the money I'd saved whilst living with her, hopefully I should be able to apply for a mortgage to buy my own place in the next year or so, which would be the icing on the cake.

I was still using the apps and enjoying my new sexual freedom. My lifestyle might seem unconventional to most people, especially for a woman my age. But I couldn't care less. After being a Stepford wife when I knew deep down it wasn't for me and trying to follow convention, I wanted to be true to myself. And the truth was, I had no interest in settling down. And I'd made a vow to only date guys who I was genuinely attracted to. I.e., no more messy, desperate, alcohol-fuelled encounters like I'd had with Terrence. After me telling him repeatedly that I wasn't interested in taking things further, he'd finally stopped messaging me.

I was currently enjoying the company of two FWBs: that's *Friends With Benefits*. And yes, they were both younger than me. Chesney was twenty-eight and Elijah was thirty-one. *And?* To quote another acronym (and I'd been using a *lot* of those lately), frankly I *DGAF*. As far as I was concerned, I wasn't doing anything wrong. We were all single. We were always safe. So why not?

See, that's the thing. Single people, especially women, are always pitied. It's like society thinks if you're not in a relationship, then you must be at home crying, knitting or surrounding yourself with dozens of cats. But that's not the case. It definitely wasn't for me. I didn't need to settle down to be happy. I could live in the moment and enjoy myself. Maybe I'd change my mind in a few months or years, but for now, I was footloose, fancy-free and I was bloody loving it!

So yes. Life was good. Everything was coming together. I was back on track. But there was just one more thing I had to do to feel totally at peace.

I checked my hair again in the mirror, swiped on some more red lippy, sat down on the sofa, then picked up my phone. There was no guarantee that this was even going to work, but I had to give it a shot.

It had been preying on my mind for the last few weeks and although I might be doing more harm than good, I didn't want to live with regrets. If it went tits up, at least I'd know I'd tried.

The phone rang once.

Then again.

And again.

And again.

I supposed it was to be expected. It had been a while. Not to mention the fact that I could have handled things a *lot* better.

It rang again.

Sometimes no answer *is* the answer.

This is silly.

I tried, but…*oh well*. Maybe it was for the best.

Just as I was about to hang up, I heard a voice. It was a bit croaky, but there was definitely someone at the other end of the line.

'He—hello?'

I looked at the phone screen. All I could see was what seemed like a white duvet cover. Or was that the ceiling?

'Finn?' I said, holding up the phone to show my face. 'Are you there?'

'Roxy?' There was a muffled sound and then some rustling as if he was trying to get a proper grip of the phone but was covering the microphone at the same time. Then the screen became clearer as he sat up and…

Oh my good God.

I had completely forgotten how fucking hot he was. I mean, I remembered he was, of course, but *jeez*…

There he was. Finn. Sitting in bed. *Topless.* With that impressive chest looking so bloody beautiful.

Lord have mercy.

He ran his fingers through his hair, showing off his bulging biceps in the process and squinted like he was trying to make me out on the screen. He looked so damn fuckable. Why hasn't teleportation been invented yet? If it had been, I would have transported myself over there and jumped on him right now.

Shit. I wasn't thinking. No wonder he was squinting. I'd been so eager to call that I'd completely forgotten about the time difference.

'Hi, Finn, sorry…did I wake you up? It's about two in the afternoon here. What time is it there?'

'Six. In the *morning*,' he groaned. His voice was still croaky and even deeper than usual. *Hose. Me. Down.*

'Bollocks! Sorry. That's not a good start, is it? I can call you back. *Later?*'

Can't believe I'd called him so early on a Saturday morning. I'd be pissed if anyone did that to me, and he probably already hated my guts after I'd blanked all of his calls, so if he put the phone down now, I wouldn't blame him.

Crap.

And what if he wasn't alone? I'd just Facetimed him without warning and he was in bed. What if some gorgeous Californian model suddenly leaned over, started stroking his chest and asked if he was ready for another round? Although I had no right to be bothered, I'd still feel pretty gutted.

I really should have thought this through before I called him. And, of course, checked the time in LA.

'I'm awake now, so tell me, what's up? Why are you calling, Roxy?'

I sat up straighter and tried to think of exactly what to say. Well, more like how to phrase it. In hindsight, it would have been better if I'd phoned rather than video called as now his hypnotic eyes were staring at me. I was looking at his chest again, and watching every movement his juicy lips were making and getting flashbacks, which was making it hard for me to concentrate. *God.* It was like, ever since he had woken up my libido, it just didn't know how to go back to sleep.

Get it together, Roxy.

The purpose of this call wasn't to drool. It was to make amends. Truth be told, I hadn't even been expecting him to answer, but now that he had, I needed to stop gawping, woman up, do what I'd set out to do and apologise. I took a deep breath.

'I'm calling, because I want to say sorry. I'm sorry that I didn't answer your calls or reply to your messages after your mum kicked me out. I should've at least wished you a safe flight or, y'know, checked you were okay. Wished you good luck in your new job. *Something*. I shouldn't have just cut you off.'

'No, Roxy. You shouldn't,' he snapped.

'But it's just that I'd lost everything. All the things that I'd worried about in the beginning, when I kept pushing you away. My job, my home, my security. Just like that, everything was gone. Ripped away. Colette was pissed off, which was understandable, and it was just a monumental shitstorm. I knew you were leaving, and you had your new job to focus on. And then when you said you thought you were starting to fall in love with me, it was just too much to get my head around. And so I just thought…I thought that the sooner we stopped talking, the sooner you'd get over me and then we could both just move on.'

He sighed, then crossed his arms. Didn't he realise that only made his pecs stand out even more, which made it harder for me to concentrate?

'I get that, but we could have still talked it through.

Like grown-ups. You were so hung up on the age thing all the time, but when it came down to it, Roxy, *you* were the one who didn't behave like an adult. Adults know that when the shit hits the fan, you don't just bury your head in the sand. You deal with it. Life is never going to be plain sailing and us being together was always a risk, I knew that. But for me, it was worth it. I told you I would handle things with my mum, so you should have trusted me. I would have smoothed things over. If you'd answered my calls, we could have stood up to her, made her see sense, and then we could have enjoyed my last week in London together, rather than both being miserable and apart.'

My heart sank. At the time, I hadn't even thought of that. I couldn't see another way out. As much as I would've wanted to, the thought of us still being able to spend time together had seemed impossible. *What a waste.*

'You're right. I see that now. I want you to know that I'm sorry, and I'd also like to say thank you. For the things that you said to your mum about me, and for helping me to get my job back. I started last Monday, and so far it's going well.'

'You're welcome, but I only spoke the truth. And, yeah, Mum told me you'd gone back.'

'So you're speaking to her again?'

'Via texts. For the moment. We'll see how it goes.'

'She loves you, you know, Finn. I don't think she realised how overbearing she was, and she explained what happened. Why she's so clingy.'

'Yeah, I get it, and I feel for her, I really do, but she has to try and change. Otherwise it's not going to work.'

'Well, I really hope it does, Finn.'

We paused and just stared at each other without saying

a word. This was actually really nice. I hadn't realised how much I'd missed him until now.

He smiled at me and then broke the silence.

'Thanks. Even though you've woken me up at this ungodly hour, it's good to talk to you. *To see you.* Clearly I look like shit, so thanks for choosing to Facetime me when I'm at my worst, but you...*you*, on the other hand, are looking mighty fine...'

Get in!

I could say I just woke up like this, but the truth was, I'd spent at least an hour on my hair and make-up before calling. *Y'know:* just to give me a bit of a boost and not at all because I wanted him to fancy me again. *Honest.*

'Well, I have to say, Finn, from where I'm sitting, you're looking pretty fine yourself,' I teased.

'*Oh really...*?' He smirked. Oh how I'd missed that smirk too. 'Well I'm very glad to hear you say that. If I was in London, I'd come straight to your flat and bend you over...'

'*Promises, promises...*' I winked.

Holy shit. I could feel my heart pumping and my undercarriage tingling. If we kept on like this, we'd be in danger of straying into filthy phone sex territory, and as much as I wanted him to pull off that duvet so that I could have a good look at his giant anaconda, I wasn't sure if that would be a good idea.

We both went silent again, like we'd realised how fast things could escalate again if we let them. Just as I started to search for the right words to help cool us down, Finn spoke.

'Listen...Rox, I get why you didn't think we could pursue things, and you're right. Both of us are still finding ourselves. My new job's going well over here, and things are getting back on track for you with your new role over there, and Mum says you're happy at your new flat too. Obviously we live thousands of miles away, and I know you're not looking for anything serious, but that doesn't mean that this has to be goodbye forever, right? I still think what we had was special.'

Despite finding it hard to admit, because I didn't like the idea of catching feelings, I knew he was right. Even though I was enjoying my booty calls with Elijah and Chesney, I realised, more so now, than ever, that the kind of chemistry I had with Finn isn't easy to come by. And I also knew that with Finn, it wasn't just the sex I liked. It was also his kindness. All the sweet things he had done for me and the fun times we'd had together. But Finn was also right: I wasn't looking for anything serious. Maybe another time, in another life, things might have been different, but it wasn't right for either of us right now. As great as I thought he was, I didn't want to get tied down. Even if I didn't have the same connection with other guys, I was still enjoying the thrills of getting up to no good.

'Yeah.' I smiled, thinking back to our escapades. 'We had a good time together. I enjoyed it. *A lot.*'

'Me too. So all I'm saying, is let's not close the door on anything completely. Let this be more of a *see you later*. It's not confirmed or anything yet, but I'm probably coming back to London at Christmas, so if it works for both of us, then maybe we can meet up again? *For old times' sake*. No strings. No sneaking around, no drama, just fun. What do you say?'

Hmm...I'm not going to lie. I *would* love to see him again and the idea of having an unfettered Finn fuck fest over Christmas was certainly appealing, but who knew what I'd be doing in two months' time? I might be busy. Doing other things…or *other people.* The fairy-tale life of a man being the ultimate goal just wasn't for me. My freedom was everything to me now, and I wouldn't give that up for anyone, not even a sex god like Finn.

'That's a tempting offer, but let's see, shall we? Play it by ear?'

'Fair enough.' He shrugged his shoulders. 'I'm okay to go with the flow. If that's what you really want?'

'Yep. No expectations, and not making any firm plans, sounds like the best plan to me.'

'Deal.' Finn smiled.

'Deal,' I replied. *Oh Christ.* If I stared at him any longer, he was going to start thawing my heart again and I couldn't be having that. No mushy stuff for me. 'Right, I'm glad everything's going well for you. It's been good to see you again, but I'd better be off. I'm meeting up with Alex.'

'Okay. Well, thanks for the call. Tell Alex I said hi, and keep in touch, yeah?'

'Yep, will do. Take care, Finn.'

'You too, Roxy,' he said, blowing me a kiss. 'You too.'

I blew him a kiss back, ended the call, then exhaled.

I was so glad I'd called. *So glad.* It could have been a disaster. But it wasn't. It was pretty cool.

I exhaled again. I felt great. *Optimistic.* Not just because Finn and I had patched things up and there was a chance of a shagathon with him at Christmas.

No.

My happiness came from realising that I was finally in control of my destiny. And my future was looking bright.

I had a job that I loved, a place of my own, I was having fun not just in the bedroom, but also outside of it because I was starting to form stronger friendships.

Take Alex, for example. We were growing closer by the day, and she'd been such a rock. Encouraging me and also giving me advice on this dating stuff. It's ironic, actually, as whilst Alex had started saying she was tired of going on the apps and having one-night stands and was desperate to find her Mr Right, fall in love and get married, I'd just started getting myself out there and was loving the lack of strings. Personally, settling down wasn't for me, but I wished her well and I was glad to be spending more time with her.

And then there was Sophia. Even though some might say I shouldn't make friends with someone who was going to be working for the company as it might muddy the waters and confuse the whole client-agency relationship, I couldn't give a toss. It was rare to find someone that I got on so well with, so I was going to continue meeting up with her outside of work. I really enjoyed our catch-ups. What she'd done with her business was so inspirational, and I reckoned on the personal front, Sophia also had some exciting adventures ahead of her, once she finally got the balls to walk away from her boyfriend, of course, and I wanted a front-row seat to see how she grew when, like me, she finally took the leap towards her freedom.

Yes. Life for me was good. In fact, more than good: it was *fucking fantastic*.

After going through so many ups and downs, and many more lows than highs, I could finally say that I was the happiest I had ever been. My *happy ever after* wasn't riding off into the sunset with a man. It was about loving myself. Choosing the path that was right for me and making my own rules. I didn't ever remember feeling so free. So independent. *So hopeful.* The world was at my feet all over again.

I had loads of exciting opportunities to pursue and I couldn't wait to see what the future had lined up for me next.

Bring it on.

GET A FREE BOOK AND EXCLUSIVE BONUS MATERIAL

Building a relationship with my readers is one of the best things about being an author. I occasionally send out fun newsletters to members of my VIP club with details of new releases, special offers, expert dating and relationship tips, interesting news and other exclusive freebies.

If you sign up to join my special VIP club, I'll send you the following, for free:

1) Yellow Book Of Love: a handy little guide, which features essential dating and relationship tips from multiple experts, including the Dating Expert of the Year 2017.

2) A list of *Alex's Top 25 Romcoms*: a definitive guide highlighting 25 top romcoms that are loved by Alex, the protagonist in my novel *Only When It's Love*. Exclusive to my VIP Club – you can't get this anywhere else.

You can get the book and the list of top romcoms, **for free,** by signing up at: www.oliviaspring.com/vip-club/

ENJOYED THIS BOOK? YOU CAN MAKE A BIG DIFFERENCE.

When it comes to getting attention for my novels, reviews are the most powerful tools in my arsenal. As much as I'd like to, I don't have the financial muscle of big New York publishers to take out full-page newspaper ads or invest in billboard posters. Well, not yet anyway!

But I *do* have something much more powerful and effective than that: **loyal readers like you.**

You see, by leaving an honest review of my books, you'll be helping to bring them to the attention of other readers and hearing your thoughts will make them more likely to give my novel a try. As a result, it will help me to build my career, which means I'll get to write more books!

If you've enjoyed *Losing My Inhibitions*, I'd be so very grateful if you could spare two minutes to leave a review (it can be as short or as long as you like) on Amazon and Goodreads or anywhere that readers visit.

Thank you so much. As well as making a huge difference, you've also just made my day!

Olivia x

Only When It's Love: Holding Out For Mr Right

Have you read my second novel ***Only When It's Love?*** It includes both Alex and Roxy from *Losin*g *My Inhibitions*, too! Here's what it's about:

Alex's love life is a disaster. Will accepting a crazy seven-step dating challenge lead to more heartbreak or help her find Mr Right?

Alex is tired of getting ghosted. After years of disastrous hook-ups and relationships that lead to the bedroom but nowhere else, Alex is convinced she's destined to be eternally single. Then her newly married friend Stacey recommends what worked for her: a self-help book that guarantees Alex will find true love in just seven steps. Sounds simple, right?

Except Alex soon discovers that each step is more difficult than the last, and one of the rules involves dating, but not sleeping with a guy for six months. Absolutely no intimate contact whatsoever. *Zero. Nada. Rien.* A big challenge for Alex, who has never been one to hold back from jumping straight into the sack, hoping it will help a man fall for her.

Will any guys be willing to wait? Will Alex find her Mr Right? And if she does, will she be strong enough to resist temptation and hold out for true love?

Join Alex on her roller coaster romantic journey as she tries to cope with the emotional and physical ups and downs of dating whilst following a lengthy list of rigid rules.

Only When It's Love **is a standalone, fun, feel-good, romantic**

comedy about self-acceptance, determination, love and the challenge of finding *the one*.

Praise For *Only When It's Love*

'**Totally unique and wonderful.** Olivia's book has a brilliant message about self-worth and brings to life an important modern take on the rom-com. Most definitely a five-star read.' - **Love Books Group**

'I guarantee **you will HOOT with laughter** at Alex's escapades whilst fully cheering her on. If you like romance, humour and a generally fun-filled read then look no further than this **gorgeous, well-written dating adventure**. Five stars.' - **Bookaholic Confessions**

'Such a uniquely told, **laugh-out-loud, dirty and flirty, addictive novel.**' - **The Writing Garnet**

'**An exciting insight into relationships in the 21st century.**' - **Amazon reader**

'With the right mix of romance and comedy, this is **the perfect read**. Five stars.' - **Love Books Actually**

'I've never read a story so quickly to find out who she would choose and if Mr Right would be the one! Five stars.' - **Books Between Friends**

'**Funny, entertaining and clever**. Olivia is an incredibly talented writer, and definitely one to watch. I cannot wait to see what she does next! Five stars.' - **BookMadJo**

'Cool, contemporary, but still wildly romantic! Yet another smasher from Olivia Spring! There's something about the way she writes that really endeared me to the heroine of this story.' - **Amazon reader**

'WOW WOW WOW!!!! *Only When it's Love* is **a dynamite love fest**. I read the entire story with the biggest smile on my face. In case you might have missed the million hints I've dropped, download the book today and jump straight in.' **Stacy is Reading**

Buy *Only When It's Love* on Amazon today!

Chapter One

Never again.

Why, why, *why* did I keep on doing this?

I felt great for a few minutes, or if I was lucky, hours, but then, when it was all over, I ended up feeling like shit for days. Sometimes weeks.

I must stop torturing myself.

Repeat after me:

I, Alexandra Adams, will *not* answer Connor Matthew's WhatsApp messages, texts or phone calls for the rest of my life.

I firmly declare that even if Connor says his whole world is falling apart, that he's sorry, he's realised I'm *the one* and he's changed, I will positively, absolutely, unequivocally *not* reply.

Nor will I end up going to his flat because I caved in

after he sent me five million messages saying he misses me and inviting me round just 'to talk'.

And I *definitely* do solemnly swear that I will *not* end up on my back with my legs wrapped around his neck within minutes of arriving, because I took one look at his body and couldn't resist.

No.

That's it.

No more.

I will be *strong*. I will be like iron. Titanium. Steel. All three welded into one.

I will block Connor once and for all and I will move on with my life.

Yes!

I exhaled.

Finally I'd found my inner strength.

This was the start of a new life for me. A new beginning. Where I wouldn't get screwed over by yet another fuckboy. Where I wouldn't get ghosted or dumped. Where I took control of my life and stuck my middle finger up at the men who treated me like shit. *Here's to the new me.*

My phone chimed.

It was Connor.

I bolted upright in bed and clicked on his message.

He couldn't stop thinking about me. He wanted to see me again.

Tonight.

To talk. About our future.

Together.

This could be it!

Things *had* felt kind of different last time. Like there was a deeper connection.

Maybe he was right. Maybe he *had* changed…

I excitedly typed out a reply.

My fingers hovered over the blue button, ready to send.

Hello?

What the hell was I doing?

It was like the entire contents of my pep talk two seconds ago had just evaporated from my brain.

Remember *being strong like iron, titanium and steel* and resisting the temptations of Connor?

Shit.

This was going to be much harder than I'd thought.

Want to find out what happens next? Buy *Only When It's Love* by Olivia Spring on Amazon now.

The Middle-Aged Virgin

Have you read my debut novel *The Middle-Aged Virgin?* It includes both Sophia and Roxy from *Losing My Inhibitions*, too! Here's what it's about:

Newly Single And Seeking Spine-Tingles…

Sophia Huntingdon seems to have it all: a high-flying job running London's coolest beauty PR agency, a lovely boyfriend and a dressing room filled with Louboutins.

But when tragedy strikes, Sophia realises that rather than living the dream, she's actually in a monotonous relationship, with zero personal life. Her lack of activity in the bedroom is so apparent that her best friend declares her a MARGIN, or *Middle-Aged Virgin*—a term used for adults who have experienced a drought so long that they can't remember the last time they had sex.

Determined to transform her life whilst she's still young enough to enjoy it, Sophia hatches a plan to work less, live more and embark on exciting adventures, including rediscovering the electrifying passion she's been craving.

But after finding the courage to end her fifteen-year relationship, how will Sophia, a self-confessed control freak, handle being newly single and navigating the unpredictable world of online dating?

If she *does* meet someone new, will she even remember what to do? And as an independent career woman, how much is Sophia really prepared to sacrifice for love?

The Middle-Aged Virgin is a funny, uplifting story of a smart single woman on a mission to find love and happiness and live life to the full.

Here's what readers are saying about it:

"I couldn't put the book down. It's **one of the best romantic comedies I've read**." Amazon reader

"Life-affirming and empowering." Chicklit Club

"Perfect holiday read." Saira Khan, TV presenter & newspaper columnist

"Absolutely hilarious! A diverse, wise and poignant novel." The Writing Garnet

Buy *The Middle-Aged Virgin* on Amazon today!

AN EXTRACT FROM THE MIDDLE-AGED VIRGIN

Prologue

'It's over.'

I did it.

I said it.

Fuck.

I'd rehearsed those two words approximately ten million times in my head—whilst I was in the shower, in front of the mirror, on my way to and from work…probably even in my sleep. But saying them out loud was far more difficult than I'd imagined.

'What the fuck, Sophia?' snapped Rich, nostrils flaring. 'What do you mean, it's over?'

As I stared into his hazel eyes, I started to ask myself the same question.

How could I be ending the fifteen-year relationship with the guy I'd always considered to be the one?

I felt the beads of sweat forming on my powdered forehead and warm, salty tears trickling down my rouged cheeks, which now felt like they were on fire. This was serious. This was actually happening.

Shit. I said I'd be strong.

'Earth to Sophia!' screamed Rich, stomping his feet.

I snapped out of my thoughts. Now would probably be a good time to start explaining myself. Not least because the veins currently throbbing on Rich's forehead appeared to indicate that he was on the verge of spontaneous combustion. Easier said than done, though, as with every second that passed, I realised the enormity of what I was doing.

The man standing in front of me wasn't just a guy that came in pretty packaging. Rich was kind, intelligent, successful, financially secure, and faithful. He was a great listener and had been there for me through thick and thin. Qualities that, after numerous failed Tinder dates, my single friends had repeatedly vented, appeared to be rare in men these days.

Most women would have given their right and prob-ably their left arm too for a man like him. So why the hell was I suddenly about to throw it all away?

Want to find out what happens next? Buy *The Middle-Aged Virgin* by Olivia Spring on Amazon.

ACKNOWLEDGEMENTS

Whoop! The acknowledgements page!

If you've read any of my other novels, you'll know how excited I get about saying thanks to all the fantastic people who made this book and my career as an author possible.

First up, I'd like to thank my A-Team of advanced readers: Mum, Jas, Jo, Loz and Brad. Thanks for being kind enough to read through the early drafts of this book and give your honest and invaluable feedback.

Thanks to my editing and design team: Eliza, Rachel, Lily and Dawn for adding extra polish and sparkle to this book and helping to make it ready to showcase to the world.

Muchas gracias to Dad, Cams and my darling PD for your continued support and encouragement.

Big thanks to the brilliant book bloggers who so generously took time out of their busy days to read and spread the word about *Losing My Inhibitions*.

And of course, to my readers. There's not enough

words in the dictionary to say how amazing you are! Three books in and the love you show me just keeps growing. I can't thank you enough for buying my novels, and for the wonderful reviews you post and your lovely messages and emails. They really mean so much.

Time to end my thank-yous already? That went quickly! I guess that's my cue to get back to writing. The next novel is already underway, so look out for a shiny new book complete with another gushing acknowledgements page coming very soon!

ABOUT THE AUTHOR

Olivia Spring lives in London, England. When she's not making regular trips to Italy to indulge in pasta, pizza and gelato, she can be found at her desk, writing new sexy chick-lit novels, whilst consuming large bowls of her mum's delicious apple crumble and custard.

If you'd like to say hi, email olivia@oliviaspring.com or connect on social media.

 facebook.com/ospringauthor

 twitter.com/ospringauthor

 instagram.com/ospringauthor

·